FORGET ME NOT

LOST & FOUND - BOOK TWO

MICHELLE DALTON

UMFANA PUBLISHERS

ACKNOWLEDGMENTS

To my husband and my boys. Love you, and thank you for your patience when I'm lost in my writing world. To all the people at Becoming Writer, or as I love to refer to you—The Write Practice, without you, I'd be lost. And to my editors Lauren and Anna at CREATING ink—you two ladies rock.

Thank you.

PROLOGUE

QUEENSLAND IN FEBRUARY IS LIKE SITTING IN A SAUNA WITH ALL your clothes on.

Isabella Irish flapped her T-shirt to and fro, hoping to create some airflow and cool off. She came to stand beneath the blooming poinciana tree which created a canopy over the open-air stage. The popular Eumundi Markets were as crowded on a Wednesday as they were on Saturdays. It'd been months since she'd visited the busy Sunshine Coast bazaar. Her stall, which had showcased her art, not too far from where she was now—before Mark had secured her first break.

Two men and three women stepped onto the stage and positioned themselves with their traditional indigenous instruments.

The earthy Australian music drifted out of a didgeridoo and flowed through her body, the player's circular breathing imitating the rain and the wind in his songs of the earth and the sky.

A hand drum soon joined in and Issi found herself

carried away to a distant place as she rode the rhythm and sound of the song.

The fog which always clouded her fractured cognizance lifted, and a clarity she had not experienced since the terrorist attack, seeped into her damaged brain. She closed her eyes and shut out the hustle and bustle around her, enjoying the brief reprieve from a mind which had lost so much.

A deep bassy tone emanated from the instrument as the player worked the mouthpiece with his breath. The sound painted a picture of the elements, and kangaroos hopping across a vista—*boing, boing*. A third instrument joined in, adding a crispness like dry grass brushed by the wind . . . it drew her away from the present an into an open space of land, her heart echoing the beat of the drum. Reds and golds unfurled around her. The music drew her back to an ancient time . . .

"Hey. You enjoying the music?" Jeff leaned in with his chin on her shoulder.

"Geez!" Issi slapped a hand to her chest as she jumped.

"Sorry, lovely." He proffered a handsome smile along with his apology.

"Yeah. It tells a story if you listen closely." She returned the gesture to show him she was okay. "Where's Sam?" She leaned past Jeff, "I can't see him." She asked her seven-foot-four ridiculously tall friend.

"Two rows down. He's discovered a stall that sells exotic food and art." Jeff rolled his eyes. "And I swear the stallholder's accent is just like yours."

"I don't have an accent." Issi waved off Jeff's odd comment. For a born-and-bred Australian, she sounded nothing like one. But her different way of pronouncing words, according to the specialist doctors, could be due to her acquired brain injury.

"Come. We need to save that man from himself. I can see him buying a truckload of foreign foods I know I won't eat. I mean, what in the holy heck is *paap*?" Jeff's lips tried to wrap themselves around the foreign word. The outcome was hilarious and Issi bit back her laughter.

He slipped an arm through hers and guided her to where Sam stood tasting food and peppering the short, plump stallholder with questions.

"Are you still tasting?" Jeff nudged his partner, who nodded and swallowed.

"This *pap* is good once you put some honey in it," he replied.

"What is it exactly?" Issi pointed to the bowl of what looked like bleached polenta.

"*Haai*. Why don't you know what pap is?" the woman's astonished expression caused Issi to pause.

Taking a step away from the table she shook her head.

"It's a maize porridge." Sam graciously drew the vendor's attention back to him. "Really, you both need to broaden your palatable horizons." He winked at Issi.

"*Ja*. So this is Achar," she said, glancing at Issi once or twice more. "And you can eat it with a lot of stuff, especially wif your *p-ah-p*." She pronounced the word slowly. "It gives it this really *lekka*... erm, *wat is nou die word vir smaak*... taste. *Ja*, taste! I make it from mango, curry..."

"Okay your accent isn't quite like that, but it shares a similarity. Even she thought you were a South African," Jeff whispered teasingly into Issi's ear, but she barely acknowledged him.

An uncomfortable sensation made itself known. As

though someone had wrapped a lasso around her midriff and was tightening it with every passing moment. Disembodied voices fought to break free from the shattered fragments of her broken brain. She'd understood the woman's foreign words—but how? And then she spotted the easel standing center to the background of the stall. On it, an artwork...

A familiarity Issi couldn't put her finger on filled her head and stirred something in her heart. The style, she knew it... but like the foreign words spoken by the stall-holder, she was not sure how.

She rubbed the scarred skin behind her left ear. The part of her brain devastated in the bomb blast ached, as though pleading with her to access what she had lost. Instead, nausea roiled in her belly and left her mouth dry and her vision blurred. Issi instinctively reached out and gripped Jeff's shoulder as her world turned.

"Lovely, are you okay?" Jeff stroked a stray lock off her cheek as Sam came to stand beside her.

"You're white as a sheet. Getting another migraine?" Sam rubbed a caring hand on her back.

Issi nodded, then pointed to the artwork. "How much?" was all she could get her stupid mouth to articulate.

1

———

Biting her bottom lip, Issi stepped away from the canvas, arching her hand so that the tip of her paintbrush pointed to the ceiling. November was turning out to be busier than she'd expected – but she could no longer ignore the urge to pick up a paintbrush. The dreams had increased in intensity over the last weeks.

After months of sculpting, Issi discovered she had awoken with a hunger for a different sort of creativity than she was used to producing. She'd eventually given in and only yesterday spent an entire morning in the art supply store in Maroochydore. She'd returned home with acrylics, two easels, and five empty canvases. She'd also been sold a container full of different sorts of brushes, cleaning materials and a really cool palette.

She was a sculptor, or at least Mark had said that was where her strengths lay, but she'd not been able to put down her brush or paints all day.

Now there were two paintings occupying the limited space in the studio of her Point Arkwright apartment.

One was her own, and the second, the painting of the

vineyard. The woman at the stall, explained it was of a vineyard back in South Africa, and that sadly the artist had been a victim of the rampant violence which scourged the nation.

It's only a beautiful piece of artwork with a sad story. That's all.

The piece she stood before now depicted the most disturbing image which had clung to her mind all these months.

Eyes. No face. No body. Only eyes. Two bold, hazel-green and gold orbs stared right into her soul. The gaze that called to her in her dream the very night after she'd bought the landscape back in February.

A spasm arched along her neck. She'd been fussing over the canvas for a few hours now and her body was tired. Issi rolled her head back in an attempt to soothe the irritated muscles, then laid her palette on the bench beside her. That was enough distraction. Today was supposed to be all about sculpting. She needed to finish two pieces. One for the Cancer Council's art auction, and the other a tiger for buyers Mark had sourced from the Middle East.

A knock at the front door distracted her as she strolled toward the basin at the far end of her work bench. She wiped her hands off with a cloth soaked in alcohol, the pungent smell burned her nose and caused Issi to sneeze.

"Who is it?" she called out from her studio as she wiped the back of her arm across her top lip, before sneezing a second time.

But there was no answer. She wasn't expecting anyone. Perhaps one of the neighbors needed something?

Issi made her way up the stairs leading to the front door from the garage-come-art-studio.

She gripped the handle but did not open it, and asked again, "Who's there?"

Silence.

An ice-cold finger trailed its way down her spine.

Standing on her tip toes and pressing her nose against the pane, Issi peeked through the window. No one. But there was something on the floor.

She twisted the lever and opened the door. On the welcome mat lay a bunch of flowers tied together with a single piece of hessian string.

Issi knelt and picked it up, then stepped out on to the landing. The bouquet of petite flowers ranged in color from deep lilac, to a snow white and bright pink. Their petals reminded her of tiny mouse ears. They smelled of early summer mornings after the first rain, and melted sugar from a sweet vendor's fudge pot. A part of her was sure she knew what sort of flowers these were, but as always, her brain failed her.

Stepping back inside her apartment, she brought the bunch to her face and took another deep whiff. Her head spun and her temples throbbed, as they did each time her fractured brain attempted to associate a lost memory with an object. Was this Mark's latest attempt to rekindle their relationship she had no memory of?

Mark Cornwall still referred to her as his fiancée, even after she'd asked him for time and space. While he'd been a pillar of support, she'd never quite been able to put to rest the gnawing sensation of discomfort when he attempted to get close to her.

When she'd regained consciousness in the hospital in Munich, Mark's was the first face she'd looked on. She'd not known who he was, but in time, as she progressed through the rehabilitation, she realized he was all she had left in this world—until she'd met Jeff and Sam, of course.

Mark was a handsome man, but Issi fought to understand why she battled to feel any attraction toward him. Though she was and always would be very grateful for him remaining by her side, even when she had probably broken his heart.

Glancing back at the bunch of flowers. *No, this isn't Mark's doing.*

He'd been in Melbourne on business this last week, and he wasn't the coy, romantic type either. His form of courtship was more forward and bold. Large bunches of roses. Expensive perfume and silky lingerie, all of which she'd never worn. How did one rekindle a flame that, as far as her grey matter was concerned, never existed?

She ran some cold water into a glass at the kitchen sink and dropped the blooms into it.

A cloying sensation gripped the back of her head. She should know what these flowers were and what they meant. She peered over her shoulder through the door of her bedroom to where her dressing table stood. Its only drawer beckoned her.

Slowly, as though she expected a snake to strike, Issi pulled open her drawer of lost yesterdays. Inside lay what was left of a badly scorched passport and a piece of jewelry Mark had often said she should get rid of. *I'll buy you a new ring when you're ready, babe.*

She gently pulled open the brittle pages of the small red booklet. Shards of burned paper and ash broke off the passport and drifted into the drawer. The photo was melted and twisted beyond recognition. She could just make out the name. *Isabella Irish*—the only form of identification found nearby after the explosion.

She'd fitted the description given by the consulate and Mark—a height of five foot three, Caucasian, blue eyes, and black hair—so the German authorities had assumed her to be Isabella Irish from 23 Deranga Drive, Applecross, Western Australia, 6153. But she didn't feel like an Isabella; she always thought of herself as Issi.

Raising her head, she met the gaze of the woman in the dressing table mirror who was so changed now, so different from no so long ago. A stronger, more determined Issi . Her fingers instinctively reached toward her damaged left ear and neck. No longer was she swathed in bandages and fear. Issi winced when she remembered how bare her scalp had felt without hair on it.

"It'll grow," Mark had assured her, and it had.

Now her hair covered the remaining scars on her scalp and was long enough to hide her disfigured ear.

Her fingers returned to the contents of the drawer.

Only one other possession had survived the bomb blast. A sapphire ring set in a white-gold princess style. Her hand shook as she reached for it. The precious metal needed polishing and a single small diamond was missing from the cluster surrounding the blue stone. Her skin prickled and her head throbbed.

Remember, Issi! She willed the dark holes of her memory to shine a light—even a glimpse would do—but only the distant throb of an oncoming headache made itself known.

"Stuff it!" She threw the damaged travel document and ring back into the dresser and slammed it closed. She had to stop looking back and learn to concentrate on the future and making new memories. "Enough!"

2

Issi regarded her unfinished sculpture of the once-famous surfer where it stood on her work bench. The two large windows she'd had built to replace the garage door and the well-placed lighting she'd had installed threw her work into great perspective. His facial features were coming together nicely and she was delighted with the form of his lips and nose. She'd give his sharp cheekbones and broad forehead attention tomorrow before she added the surf-board and other details. Gosh, she loved the feeling of the cool sculpting clay beneath her fingertips.

When she'd first been commissioned to sculpt a piece for the auction, she'd had no idea what would be suitable. Then she'd stumbled across the surfing competition held at Mudjimba one weekend. It had been in honor of a surfer who'd recently passed away from a melanoma. She approached his family and received permission to base her piece on him. His life story and dedication to the sport had instantly filled her with inspiration.

Issi placed her modeling spatula on her bench. It was time for a chai at Jeff and Sam's place. The painting in the corner called to her, but Issi ignored it. It filled her with too many unanswered questions, ones she simply was not in the mood to confront right now.

She flipped off the light switch and trotted up the stairs.

After a quick shower, Issi lathered on sunscreen, and dressed in her walking shorts, T-shirt, and trainers. She slipped her phone and key card into a sleeve strapped around her arm, then grabbed her cap and pulled it onto her head, making sure her shoulder-length curly mop hid what needed hiding.

She was still not used to people's reactions to the melted, contorted skin on her neck and left ear.

The flowers, which sat smiling in the glass where she'd placed them the day before, caught her attention and a strange sensation rippled along her neck. She walked over to them and sniffed. A laugh, deep and gravely, echoed through her mind. A flash of a brownstone building hugged by shrubs adorned in the same flowers knocked her backward.

What the . . . She closed her eyes and tried to grab a hold of the image. But it was gone. Frustrated, she gripped the flowers harshly and ripped them from their makeshift vase then dropped them into the bin.

Issi slammed her front door shut then stomped her way down the steps and along the brick walkway to the wall hugging their small estate. It was a glorious afternoon.

Waving the key card, she pushed the wrought-iron gate open. She double checked the road for any cars before jogging across to the boardwalk. The council had built the wooden path which snaked its way along the Jubilee Esplanade and in to Coolum Beach more than a year ago— one of their better ideas.

Issi took a moment to appreciate the ocean.

Steam rose off the cerulean waters in waves of mist and the sun beat down on her—it was going to be a hot November. She rolled her head back and shrugged her shoulders. A soft thrum in the base of her neck warned of another headache—another matter the doctors were unable to resolve.

Her thoughts drifted in and out with the waves. It was a good day to swim. The sea was calm, almost flat, and there were no rips causing troubles for swimmers and lifeguards alike. But she was on her way to grab a much-needed chai and catch up with her best mates.

The coast was busier now. More moms with prams and joggers in the latest gym gear, families with boogie boards, and kids on scooters.

"Hey!" she called out as a teenager zipped past her on his skateboard.

The popular Sunshine Coast was filling up for the Christmas holidays. Already the influx of traffic along Jubilee Esplanade was noticeable. Issi huffed as she came to stand at the traffic lights across the way from her destination. The walk had gotten her blood pumping, and her stiff muscles loosened. The cafés brimmed with recognisable faces and tourists alike. There was a decent queue working its way out of Jeff and Sam's Place too. Slipping past the waiting customers, Issi stepped inside the establishment. It hummed with the laughter and quiet chatter of patrons. A middle-aged surfer called out, "Yo, Jeff, tell that man of yours in the kitchen, this is the best lobster bisque on the coast!"

She removed her sunglasses and cap, swooshing a hand through her ringlets but being careful not to lift any hair away from her left ear. The cool breeze created by the ceiling fans washed over her, and the Beach Boys version of

"Christmas Day" played from the speakers. It wasn't a memory, but some part of her knew that this was her favourite time of year. The mood was jovial and relaxed. She loved the guys' vintage taste.

Their music, clothing, and even the décor, was that of a sixties beachfront café.

"Hello, lovely." Jeff waved from behind the counter. His sun-bleached tresses were tied in a bun on his head.

A few wisps dangled out over his ears and Issi smiled when she caught some nearby customers following his every movement with focused intent. The flex of his broad shoulders showed beneath his tight surf-branded T-shirt as he worked and moved around behind the bar. "The usual?"

"Yes thanks." She nodded before making her way to her spot of shade on the deck. The small round table and single chair stood in a corner away from the crowds, and always carried a *reserved* label.

She'd asked them not to make a fuss, especially in the silly season when they could do with an open chair and table. But the boys had refused. She appreciated their kindness.

She'd met the two of them at her first exhibition in Noosa. They'd been almost inseparable since.

"It's gonna be a scorcher." Jeff winked as he placed the tall steaming chai in front of her. "Hungry?"

"No thanks." She met her friends gaze then turned to her mug. A Santa carrying a surfboard had been painted on the side.

"Oh, you've got that look about you," he said, wagging a finger at her.

"Yeah, and what look's that?" Heat rushed over her neck and cheeks.

"The one that says you've done something amazing. What's up?"

"I've been painting," she whispered, not sure why she was afraid of anyone else overhearing.

Jeff promptly pulled out a chair from the table behind him and sat. "Painting? My, my, you are a woman of many talents."

Issi leaned forward. "Ever since the markets . . ." Her head twisted left then right as her eyes grazed over the tables nearby, then focused on Jeff. "I've had this dream and when I wake up, all I can remember are a pair of eyes." She swallowed hard then took a deep breath.

The memory had not eased in the ensuing months but grown in intensity. Like a person trapped on the other side of a locked door, it banged against her brain. Problem was, she didn't have the key. Fear and frustration bit into her nerves just speaking about it.

"Why are we whispering?" Jeff folded his strong arms across his chest.

Issi swallowed hard then tried to smile. "I don't know."

He placed a reassuring hand on her arm. "I can't wait to see it!"

"But I've still got two sculptures to finish. I don't have time for this distraction."

"You do if it helps you remember. Besides, I haven't seen you this excited in weeks—that's a plus in my book." He smiled.

"Yeah . . . but . . ."

"Stop stressing. You're going great with the new pieces, and soon, you're gonna be the coast's hottest commodity! Why not enjoy the diversity of your creativity while you're at it?"

"Oh, Jeff." She smiled and flapped her hand at her

friend. "Will you both come 'round after closing this afternoon? I need your objective eyes and some good company."

"Absolutely!"

A customer rang the service bell, drawing Jeff's attention away from her.

"Coming!" he called over his shoulder before he made his way back to the counter.

Issi picked up her chai and sipped.

Her mate was right. She was stressing about nothing, and Mark would have to make peace with the fact that she also enjoyed painting. The two skills fed each other, quickened her inspiration, and added to the beauty of her creations.

Issi sat back and enjoyed the vibe. Across the busy road, the beach spread out like a hot golden blanket edged in a turquoise and white lace as the waves rolled in and trickled away. Families frolicked in the summer sun, and Issi envied their perfect bliss.

A man came to sit at the table closest to her just as the breeze shifted to a south-easterly. The scent of his cologne drifted across the way. Musk lined with subtle hints of sage and lavender stormed her olfactory receptors.

Her mind bucked and bolted like a wild colt, then stumbled, leaving her heart trembling in the corner of her chest. And her brain did that thing again. The world around her froze and she had the sensation of lost fragments desperately pressing at the edges of her mind.

Issi shifted in her seat as her glance travelled toward the stranger. He was handsome with sandy-blond cropped hair and a strong, stubbled jaw. There was something about the way he sat . . . or was it his face and the way he folded his arms?

His cheeks appeared drawn, as though he'd been ill. His

eyes hid behind a pair of sunglasses, masking most of his expression.

As though he could feel her staring at him, he turned his head and nodded, and the corners of his mouth turned up. A dimple sitting on the cleft of his chin made itself known and caused her insides to flip.

A juggernaut of ghosted somethings bombarded her insides and collided with the numb, blank parts in her head. The deep laughter from this morning when she'd smelled the flowers reverberated across her mind as an invisible hand fisted her diaphragm and squeezed the air from her lungs.

The space around her formed invisible walls which threatened to close in on her. She needed space and quiet to figure out what was going on with her.

Leaving her chai unfinished, she rushed out of the café.

"Where you running off to?" Jeff's voice echoed across the busy café.

But all she managed in reply was to mimic sculpting as she proffered the best *see ya later* smile she could muster. If this was a déjà vu moment—she didn't think she liked it.

Issi took off in a sprint down the outside steps and onto the pavement, skidding to a halt at the red pedestrian light. Laughter and too many holidaymakers crowded her. Her heart continued to pound the inside of her chest and bile burned the lining of her tummy. Humid sea air turned to sharp icicles in her throat and sweat trickled down her cheeks.

Was it the combination of the dimple and his smile? Or was it those subtle notes of spice and man that triggered something buried beneath all the scar tissue in her brain?

The light turned green and Issi slipped in and out

between people strolling and chatting as she sprinted across the road and headed along the boardwalk.

Her mind drifted again to the flowers and the painting. She'd been searching for so long, pleading with her grey matter to heal, to remember, and then she'd begun to give up. Why now? The dreams, the flowers, this stranger. A flutter of excitement came to rest beside the panic which now flooded her system.

She stopped at the top of the lookout. It was quieter here. The ebb and flow of water below began to soothe her nerve-wracked insides. Leaning with her hands against the wood palings that separated her from a sheer drop to the beach far below, Issi inhaled until her lungs felt as though they would burst, then slowly let the breath go. She stepped back and lowered her head as the hurricane of anxiety within her began to subside. Dammit! She should have approached the man instead of bolting—but fear was a wicked beast when it dug its claws into you. Then a thought made itself known – had Mark changed his brand of after-shave before the bombing? Why had the smell of this man affected her so?

Tears burned the back of her eyes. Would she ever find the answers she wanted? She'd honestly thought she'd made peace with her empty past—she'd tried to. Did the key to this sudden return in fragmented memory lie within that painting? With Mark and his old brand of cologne?

Deep breaths, Issi.

In and out. You're overthinking it.

Her arm began to vibrate, snapping her out of her trance. She pulled her phone from the pocket strapped around her bicep.

Think of the devil and you stand on his tail...

"Hey, babe." Mark's voice crooned through the earpiece.

"Hi."

"You okay? You sound a little out of breath."

Issi shut her eyes and tried to center her thoughts. "Fine. I'm just out for a stroll."

"How you going with the work? Don't forget I need that tiger by the end of the week—and how's the Pratta?"

Typical Mark. Straight to business.

"I'm on track," she fibbed. There was a muttering in the background, a language which she was not familiar with. "Where are you?"

"At the Sheraton." His reply was cool and short, sparking a warning in the back of her mind.

"Oh, okay." It'd been a quiet week with Mark away in Melbourne. One of her sculptures had sold at the well-known White Sails gallery and he'd gone to close the deal and take a second sculpture of a fisherman for them to exhibit. He also had other artists' work to deal with.

"I have two more clients to see and then I'll be on the next flight home."

An uncomfortable silence hovered between them before his voice, edged in its usual softness, drifted into her ear. "I love you. Don't forget that."

Issi nodded, forgetting he couldn't see her. "Chat later. Have a safe trip."

She was unable to return the sentiment. Would she ever be able to reciprocate his feelings?

Wasn't love something which came easily? If they'd really been as inseparable as he so often told her, wouldn't her feelings have remained? How much longer could she lie to herself?

3

Issi sat on the couch, sketch pad on her lap, charcoal in hand. After the shock of whatever it was that had happened at the café and a slow walk home from the look out, her fingers itched to create. She stared out at the ocean in the distance and allowed the unsettling memory of the afternoon to steady in her mind's eye.

She deftly guided the edge of the charcoal across the white surface. A face, not so much the man, but his smile, came to life on the blank page. The piece of burned wood pinched between her thumb and forefinger followed the curve of his lips and the memorable dimples which appeared on his chin like the first stars in the evening heavens. Her strokes easily brought to life the prominent features swirling around in her head like a vortex in open space.

Had she once known someone with similar features? A friend, and old boyfriend from school – because this man was surely not someone from her past, or he'd have recognized her.

Issi shaded the left angle of his jaw. Her fingers moved to

sketch his eyes and froze—she'd not seen them as they'd sat behind a pair of shades.

A sharp rap on the door drew her away from her drawing.

She closed her pad and stood to answer it.

Jeff and Sam greeted her with boyish grins and a large platter of food at her front door.

"Hey, guys. All done for the day?" She flicked open the lock on her screen door and stepped back to allow them in.

"Your cryptic hand signals as you ran looked like a flapping Magpie," Jeff placed a kiss on her forehead, then made his way to her kitchen. "If I didn't know you better, I would have thought you were off to chase a cyclist."

Issi chuckled.

"Yeah. The chai that bad, girl?" Sam added kissing her cheek.

"Naw, it's those garish Christmas mugs you have me serve them in." Jeff winked.

"Ha ha ha. Oh, you two. Sorry. I was trying to imitate sculpting by the way." She repeated the movement.

"Ooooh! Yeah, nah, try words next time." Sam flapped his hands and bobbed his head like a bird, and they all burst out laughing.

"I should have explained. I think I had a... memory blitz . . . of sorts." She rubbed the area behind her ear then closed the door.

"A memory blitz? This is new." Jeff placed the platter on her kitchen counter. He walked over and wrapped a thick, muscled arm around her and pulled her into him. If she'd had a brother in her previous life, she hoped he would have been just like him.

Jeff the protector. Jeff the unconditional acceptor, always there no matter how bad his own day had been.

"Not really. It started that day at the markets when I bought the artwork."

"I knew it was more than a migraine." Sam exclaimed as he bumped a fist off the kitchen counter.

"Yeah. I swear it felt as though someone cracked my head open like an egg and poured scrambled yolk back into it. Anyway, the painting, it spoke to me in a way I can't explain." Issi followed the guys out to her balcony and flopped down in a chair as they placed the platters, glasses and wine down on the glass surface of her outdoor table.

"Who's the artist?" Jeff asked opening his phone.

"Van Rooyen." She stopped when the guys gave her an odd look. "What?" she shrugged confused.

"You pronounce it in the same accent that woman spoke in," Jeff said softly, as though he were tiptoeing around a sleeping fairy.

"Oh. I think the stallholder told me and I just remember it." She swallowed back a sliver of fear, knowing the woman had done no such thing.

"Well, here he is. Wow—such a sad story. He lived down in South Australia for a bit before he returned to his wine farm in South Africa where he was shot and killed." Jeff turned his phone to give Sam and herself a good look.

"Anything?" Sam asked when Issi took Jeff's phone and scrolled through the article her friend had found on a South African news website.

"Nup. Nothing." She shook her head. "It says here, *he was survived by two children and a wife he'd left behind in Australia.* That is sad." She handed the phone back to Jeff.

"Huh." Jeff closed the window and put down his phone, then sipped his wine.

"Is it possible the style might be familiar and it's triggering a memory, but you really don't know the artist?" Sam leaned forward and grabbed a smaller plate before loading it with food.

"Yes. Just like this afternoon at the café – the man who sat opposite me." She sipped her wine then rolled her head back to try and relieve some of the tension building at the base of her neck.

"What man, where?" Sam shifted forward on his chair.

Issi allowed herself to remember the subtle tickle of sandalwood and lavender settling on her neurons before she described the man and how his appearance had unnerved her.

"And that's what had you running?" Jeff cocked his head.

"Yup. It stirred a memory, just like those stupid flowers." She waved a hand toward the kitchen.

"You know what kind they are, right?" Sam twisted open the lid of the wine and began to pour.

"No." Issi shook her head.

"Forget-me-nots." He watched her intently.

His words filled her heart with a cold trickle of unquantifiable emotions. The unease which had swept over her that afternoon returned and a thin film of sweat erupted from her skin. "Oh," she mumbled as she chewed on the significance of the petite mouse-eared blooms.

"And the painting... what if you owned one of them before . . . you know, before the... accident." Jeff's sheepish gaze brought a smile to her face.

"The bombing, Jeff. You can call it that."

"I know. But it always sounds so violent." He fingered the food on his plate, picking up a crab stick and shoving it in his mouth.

Issi smiled. Sometimes it was hard even for her to believe she'd survived something one only ever saw on the television.

"Well, everything was destroyed in a house fire before we returned from Munich. All Mark could save was that one photo of my parents. All my previous work, books—everything is gone. So, I have no idea."

Sam sighed and rubbed his chin with his right hand, "Ask Mark. Surely he'd know what art you owned before the fire?"

"Hmm. Yeah I guess it couldn't hurt."

Mark had taken her to see the charred residence that, like her mind, it had offered no answers to her lost past. How much bad luck could one person endure? She'd survived a terrorist attack and then, thanks to an electrical fault, a week before their return her home was no more.

"I have a lot of questions for him, actually." She said more to herself than her mates.

"Aren't you a little freaked out? I mean, somebody left you flowers with no note," Sam added with a half-full mouth.

"Seriously, swallow before you speak, babe." Jeff handed Sam a serviette.

"Yes and no. Does that make me weird? Naive?" She sat up straight, almost spilling her wine.

"No. It makes you vulnerable. Love, I think you're over-thinking this," Jeff's chocolate gaze grew darker and the creases between his eyes deepened.

"But I know that they mean something, and that scares the shit out of me."

For a moment, Issi focused on the love which wrapped itself around her friends. Jeff and Sam were the dream couple. They complemented each other in every way lovers should. But unlike all the other times she'd admired their closeness, this evening she felt a different emotion stir—envy. She envied her mates their love. A cold emptiness stirred in her chest, as though she'd lost something incredibly important, but didn't know what it was.

She shifted in her chair and turned toward the ocean, across the way from where they sat. It was a glorious dusk. The disappearing sun's hot red fingers reached out like strobe lights across the heavens from the west to the east, coloring the sky in crimsons, magenta, and bronze. The humidity intensified the colors.

Utopia.

"It's been a heck of a day for that traumatized brain of yours, huh?" Sam poured the last of the wine into their glasses. "Please eat." He nodded toward the platter.

Issi smiled and picked up a cracker laden with blue cheese.

An electric silence wrapped itself around the trio. The guys had been there for her through thick and thin. Her life would have been so lonely without them.

"You want to try that thing where you close your eyes and . . ." Sam began to suggest.

She shook her head. "I have. All I see is... you'd better come with me" She waved for them to follow as she led them down to her studio.

"Wow, lovely. Is this is Cologne and Smiles guy? He has no eyes." Jeff pointed out as he gripped the pad.

"Yes but that's not what I wanted to show you."

"These are fantastic!" Sam called out.

Jeff left the sketch and trotted toward the area Sam was standing.

"Winner, winner!" Sam clapped his hands together. "It's definitely a masterpiece. Pity you'll not see a cent of this one's sale." He pointed toward the Pratta. "'Cause believe me, it's gonna break the buyer's bank."

Issi rolled her eyes at Sam. "I don't care that it's for charity, and all the better if it rakes in the dosh."

Jeff walked around the bench to get a three-sixty impression of both artworks. "Where do you get your ideas and inspiration from, lovely?"

"So many things. Dreams, a story, a word . . . I'm not like others who have one specific thing they can pinpoint and say, 'It's this or that,'" she replied and shrugged.

The tiger she was creating was definitely a turning point for her art. She'd loved sculpting the paws, and the lithe muscled features of its torso and legs—it wasn't your usual conservative-looking piece as she'd added a lot of color and glass.

"And this?" Jeff turned toward the canvas of the eyes. "Is it the painting you were telling me of earlier?"

Issi nodded and joined her mates as they all considered the half-finished canvass.

"It's eerie," Sam whispered.

"They're gorgeous." Jeff reached out and stroked an index finger down the left spine of the canvas.

"I've dreamed of them every night since last week," Issi added.

Sam shivered and Jeff gripped his shoulder. "Perhaps it's nothing more than an idea taking form?"

"Perhaps." Issi shoved her hands into her short pants pockets. *Perhaps not.* There was more to it than merely an idea.

"Come, there's an entire platter to finish and some more wine. You know how much I hate to waste." Sam beckoned from the foot of the studios steps.

Issi almost bumped in to Jeff when paused by the bench and glanced at her sketch of the man.

"Something the matter?" Sam asked.

Jeff opened his mouth, then clamped it shut and shook his head as a shudder wracked his limbs. "Just a thought. But I'm being silly."

———

Issi waved a last goodbye as Sam and Jeff drove away, then locked her gate and shut her door. She grabbed two headache tablets from the bottle standing on the corner of her kitchen bench and swallowed them with a handful of water from the tap before making her way back to the balcony. The tension in her neck was morphing into a thrumming in her head.

The calm waters of late dusk had morphed into a tumbling black trimmed with angry froth. The sickle moon shone a little brighter and the stars twinkled as they blessed the earth with their sparkly smiles. The memory of lavender and sandalwood dragged her back to the afternoon and the strange man.

"That's all he is, Issi—a stranger wearing expensive cologne," she whispered to herself.

She took a deep slow breath, held it, and let it go. It was exhausting, this constant weight pushing on her soul. There was no need to remember the past, was there? If it had any importance to who she was now, it would have come in search of her. Wouldn't it?

The eyes in her portrait were coincidence – a burst of inspiration brought on by a crazy dream. They didn't belong to either of her parents. In the photo recovered from the fire, the man who'd been her father had owned deep-set chocolate-brown eyes and her mother, a lighter shade of blue than hers. She hated that an act of pure hatred had robbed her of all memory and emotions connected to them, and to a man she was supposed to love.

Issi searched her heart but there was no love or loss over the couple who'd supposedly raised her. She'd been to visit their graves only once before leaving Western Australia, had searched for other relatives, with Mark's assistance, but found no one. Her life had consisted of art and Mark before, as it did now.

The Isabella Irish of the past didn't have any personal social media accounts, except for her artist page and Instagram account which Mark managed. Her phone and laptop had been destroyed in the bombing and no images of herself had been posted on her pages—only her art. Something she'd continued to do.

Mark had shown her a handful of photos of them together on his phone. But something about the pictures had always looked out of place. There was a photo of her with longer hair and a brighter smile standing wrapped in Mark's arms at a barbeque in Bali, with friends she'd not met since. To most people it was a beautiful photo, but to her keen eye something was wrong. When she'd asked about the friends, Mark had simply shrugged and said, "We should go back sometime and visit."

A second image on his phone was from the day they'd gotten engaged on a beach. But like the Bali image, it struck her as slightly off-center, though she was unable to pinpoint why.

Eventually she'd stopped questioning it all and worked on making peace with it.

Mark was all she had; there was no one else. Not a single soul but him to help her fill in the gaps. While she considered Jeff and Sam family, they had no link to who she was before.

Issi returned to her studio; she still had work to do. But instead of working on the Pratta, she found herself staring at the two canvases. The eyes and the landscape.

The painting of the eyes comforted the hollow pit of emptiness that threatened to pull her down into a null void she was falling into. Like a dream, precious, deep, forgiving and unconditional in its love, the paintings warm glow made her feel safe. She had no idea who they belonged to, but she didn't care. She simply loved that she was able to bring them to life on her canvas.

Grabbing a small piece of charcoal, Issi leaned in and scribbled her signature in the bottom left corner, *II.*

"Perfect," she uttered when her phone rang.

"Babe." Mark's voice quickly reminded her of the work she should be doing and not the painting that had distracted her from it.

"Hi, Mark."

"I've just landed and am on my way to you." His voice conveyed his eagerness and Issi's mood swung from thoughtful to anxious.

"I've had a big day in the studio," she fibbed.

"Great! I can't wait to see how far you are. Our time is running out. My client in Qatar called a few minutes ago for an update on the tiger. Perhaps you can take a photo so I can text him and set him at ease?"

Issi swallowed back her annoyance. Yes, she had to finish and yes, her time was running out. But, she didn't need him reminding her. "You know I don't do that, Mark. My work remains mine until it is in the hands of the buyer. It needs one more layer of glaze. Why don't you come around tomorrow at lunchtime and look?"

"Oh. I thought I'd grab a bottle of red and we could

catch up?" The disappointment in his tone almost caused her to give in.

"I'm not good company now. But bring it along tomorrow and we can share it over lunch?" She tried to sound less irritable and more loving.

"Sure. It'll be good to see you again." He sounded cold; she didn't blame him.

"I'll order in?" her left hand pinched the bridge of her nose as her eyes scrunched closed.

"No, I'll take you to lunch. We need to pop past the gallery in any case, so keep your day open. We can leave after you've shown me the sculptures."

"Erm . . . okay. See you then," Issi replied, not liking the commanding tone that had snuck into his voice.

She put down the phone and sat on the only chair in her studio. She reached back and massaged her neck. The headache was getting worse.

Why couldn't she feel the way he did?

It would be so wonderful to be held, and cherished. To love and be loved. But when she imagined Mark doing that, her skin crawled and her mind balked. Why?

Her gaze found its way back to her painting of the eyes —her insides flipped and she shook her head.

Issi slipped off the chair and stepped toward it. She lifted it off the easel and returned upstairs to her lounge where she placed it against the wall. There was a cool breeze drifting off the ocean and into her apartment through the open patio doors. She'd sleep here tonight. The fresh air would help take the edge off the acceleration of the throbbing in her head.

But first she needed a shower. The cool water would wash away the niggling drumroll in her skull. She crossed the index and forefinger of her right hand. *No migraine, please?*

Issi strolled out of the bathroom wrapped in a towel, her hair dripping. She sat down in front of the mirror of her dressing table.

She traced a finger along her hairline and pulled back her damp curls. She allowed her finger to continue tracing its way along the thick angry scar, which ran from the back of what remained of her ear to the base of her skull. She gently stroked what was left of her earlobe. The surgeons had done a stellar job with the reconstruction but it was still a mangled piece of flesh. Her hearing was no longer as good in her left as it was in her right, but thankfully not to the extent that she needed a hearing aid.

She dropped her hair in place, leaned toward the mirror, glared into her dark blue eyes, and willed her brain to find its way back to the past. Memories fought to break free from their restraints. She could feel them reaching out from their dark prison. She pushed harder as a hot spear of pain pierced the top of her skull. She winced but did not retreat.

"Who are you?"

4

WAVES CRASHED ONTO THE SHORE. THEIR ANGRY ROARS echoed across the beach and through the open balcony door.

Issi pushed herself off the floor where she'd fallen asleep staring at her painting.

The sea had evolved overnight to a raging beast with dirty white spines edging the crests of waves. It raced up and bit into the shore, gulping mouthfuls of sand, shells, and debris whilst warning bathers to remain on dry land.

She stood for a moment, her mind foggy, her gaze mottled by sleep and hazy, humid air.

Coffee.

She needed coffee. And then she had work to do.

Her neck felt looser and the war drums pounding a broken war cry had receded to a soft thrum in the back of her skull.

Today would see her add the final layer of glaze to the tiger. Excitement buzzed through the marrow of her bones. It was always nerve-wracking allowing the world a glimpse of what went on in her soul. That was what her art was—

her innermost being sculpted and carved into solid form for all humanity to gaze at. It was both terrifying and exhilarating all at once.

As soon as she'd painted a last layer of glaze on the tiger, she started on the Pratta. The sculpture portrayed the surfer from a photo his family had given her. He stood tall and smiling, wearing surf shorts and hugging his surfboard. With his facial features and hair done, it was time to emphasize the tawny toned arms, abdomen, and legs of the Queensland surfing legend.

A knock at the front door distracted her. She raced up the stairs.

"Who's there?" She gripped the door handle, but didn't turn it.

Silence whispered a desolate reply. Her gate was locked, so with care, she opened the door. No one except . . .

On the welcome mat, there was a bunch of forget-me-nots. Her stomach flipped and her breath caught in her chest. Who were they from?

She unlocked her gate and stared in both directions. No one. She picked up the blooms and sniffed them. The scent of summer and sugar dazzled her. A warm gooey cloud bloomed in the center of her chest—the way those dark mulberry clouds on the horizon did on hot summer afternoons, threatening thunder and devastating winds.

Issi sniffed the flowers a second time and a sense of nostalgia flooded every cell in her body. *What the . . .?*

Instead of the anxiety that had ensnared her when she experienced a memory blitz , happiness and laughter, her own laughter, embraced her and dared her to want more. To need more . . . the feeling began to fade when logic stepped in. Her smile fell from her face and her laughter died.

Should she care that some unknown person was leaving flowers at her front door?

"Who is this from?" She shoved the hand holding the bunch out in front of her, calling to the empty doorway before her.

Dammit. Whoever left it here can't have gotten far.

Issi searched for the part of her that should be frightened, instead anger and frustration flared inside of her. "This isn't funny!" What if it was simply a kind neighbor's gesture? She should be careful nonetheless.

She stepped back and locked both the gate and front door before walking to the kitchen. She paused at the bin, her toe on the lid's peddle. But something inside her stopped her from dropping them into the garbage. Instead, she made her way to the sink and grabbed a glass before pouring some tap water and dropping the bunch in.

Issi considered the name of the pretty little indigo, white, and pink flowers. Was it a coincidence they were called forget-me-nots?

Her eye caught the clock on her kitchen wall.

No time to ponder now.

———

"Magnificent!" Mark Cornwall's hazel eyes gleamed, the corners of his mouth reaching each ear. "This is certainly the best work you have produced yet."

He turned and pulled Issi into him, laying an unexpected kiss on her cheek. "You are my golden goose, darling."

Issi tried to free herself from his embrace. "I'm pleased you like it."

"Like it? I bloody love it! And so will the buyers." He

lifted her off her feet and spun her around. Mark was a decent five-foot-nine, with dark brown hair, and a looker—if you went for his sort.

Issi couldn't help but squeal. His excitement was a bit infectious and she was incredibly proud of her work.

He came to a stop and leaned toward her.

Panic surged through her body. It didn't feel right. Whenever they got caught in the moment, an alarm would sound somewhere in the back of her mind. She imagined the same sensation would awaken if she were to cheat on a husband or partner.

Issi didn't want to upset him, nor did she want to give him any indication she wanted more. She had to get out of the situation. So, she faked a sneeze on his shoulder. He let go at once and pulled a hanky from his pants pocket, then wiped his collar.

"I've been very patient, Isabella. Can't you see how much I care? How well we are suited? I mean . . ." He pinned her to the spot with a look that said he'd reached his fill. "Do you know of any other fiancés who would wait in the shadows for nearly two years the way I have?" Mark stepped toward her and snaked an arm around her waist.

There was no reprieve as he lowered his head toward hers. Perhaps if she just gave a little, moved beyond the unknown . . . maybe allowing him in would bridge the gap and remind her heart of what they'd once shared?

The smell of expensive cologne and peppermint enveloped Issi as his lips touched hers. They were cold and hard. His hand roamed from the small of her back and over her buttock, the other cupping her neck as his tongue entered her mouth.

Her heart raced and it was not in the hungry sort of way it should have been.

Issi's instinct was to bite down, but her better judgment told her there was an easier way to end this without drama. She repositioned her hands and prepared to pull away when his phone rang. Mark's grip on her tightened then let go and he drew back and reached into his jacket pocket.

Issi smiled and swallowed her relief, loving the person who'd created the old cliché about being saved by the bell.

"Dessi, darling." Mark made to pull her back in.

But Issi shook her head and pointed to his phone as she slipped out from his grasp and ran up the steps, only too grateful to make it out of the studio and into the openness of her apartment. She had to talk this through with him. Now more than ever she knew there was no future for them as a couple. How he would take it was a different matter entirely.

"We're on our way. I can't wait to show you a snapshot," Mark said as he stood on the top step, giving Issi a cheeky grin. He knew she hated photos of her unfinished work. Was this payback for earlier?

———

MARK SPED down the esplanade and onto David Low Way.

"Slow down, Mark. There're kids everywhere." Issi gripped the sides of the plush leather seats as he zoomed through a roundabout, barely taking time to look for oncoming traffic.

"This is a road for cars. Kids shouldn't be allowed near them," he growled, then pressed on the multi-buttoned steering wheel of his luxury German sedan. The speakers sprang to life with the rapid beat of the latest electronic dance song. "DJ Medusa," Mark shouted to her over the ruckus which invaded the car and thrashed her eardrums.

Issi sighed inwardly as they finally pulled into the

parking lot. The space sat right behind the gallery which faced the main street of the affluent beach town of Noosa. Mark switched off the car and his erratic music died with the engine. Her ears hummed with relief.

She swung open the door before Mark could do or say anything else in the private space of his vehicle. She trotted toward the sidewalk then waited for him to catch up.

"Come. Dessi's waiting." Mark strutted toward her, grabbed her hand and hurried off down the walkway with Issi in tow.

Like Coolum, Noosa was full of tourists, locals, and shoppers. They passed one or two designer beachwear stores and a new restaurant owned by the runner-up of a previous year's TV chef competition. The queue outside was twice that of her mates' café.

Clear glass doors wearing a single horizontal sand-blasted pattern slid open and the pristine air-conditioned atmosphere of the gallery welcomed Issi as the pair stepped inside. On an easel, balanced a painting of a local artist Issi admired.

Emily Kame Kngwarreye was a prolific and very successful indigenous artist. She'd painted many contemporary indigenous works, one of which stood smiling back at Issi now. Unfortunately, she wasn't gifted time to admire the bold colors and shapes of the Utopia community artist...

"Isabella. Mark! Oh, I am so happy to see you." A woman whose height relied solely on the courtier stilettos she wore pranced toward them from a back office. Her dark red lips were stark against her pale made-up face, matching her fire truck red hair.

"Dessi, darling." Mark took both the woman's proffered hands in his before planting a kiss on either cheek.

"Mark says your sculpture for the auction is almost complete?" She spoke but barely looked at Issi, her cool grey gaze remaining focused on Mark. Issi couldn't help but wonder —if she really was hung up on Mark, wouldn't she feel a little threatened by the attention the pair were giving one another?

"Oh, yes. I snuck a photo just before we left this morning." Mark finally let go of Desire's hand to pull out his phone and show her. The pair crooned over the photo then Mark said, "Babe. Stay here while I sort out the deets for the auction with Dessi."

Issi nodded and plastered on her best smile as they disappeared into the office. Why had he even bothered dragging her along?

Well she had no problem entertaining herself. There were some gorgeous pieces here, all from locals, and a handful from better-known, now-long-since-passed-on artists like Emily.

A weird chill ran the length of Issi's spine. She spun on her heel, froze and searched the walkway on the other side of the pristine windows of the gallery. The sidewalk was full of people, so why did she get the feeling she was being watched?

———

"Thanks." She passed the delivery man the money and took the bags with food in them. Mark had dragged her to three different restaurants, all full, all with a waiting list and eventually decided they'd get take-aways. She didn't close the door this time but left both it and the gate wide open. She couldn't explain it, but for the first time since Munich, she didn't feel comfortable alone with Mark.

She had suggested the guys' place, but Mark had flat-out refused.

He made no effort to help as she unpacked the two cardboard boxes from the paper bag and placed his on the counter, while he unbuttoned the jacket of his expensive suit, hung it over the back of the kitchen stool then proceeded to roll up both sleeves before sitting.

Mark rarely showed flesh. On the inside of his left arm was a tattoo. A red arrow. She'd only ever seen it once before and when she'd asked him about it, he'd simply brushed it off as a drunken mistake.

With a fork in one hand and his phone in the other, he began to munch on his kale and salmon salad.

Jeff had once remarked that men like Mark were all about themselves, but if he really was, wouldn't he have left her after the bombing?

Issi opened her container and delighted in the savory fragrance of the roti and Thai chicken green curry—she'd tackle the issue that was *them* once she got some wholesome food in her belly. Issi scooped up a mouthful of rich, spicy curry using a piece of roti and shoved it into her mouth.

Mmmm, this is so good.

The kaffir lime and cilantro complemented the shallots and chili, with just enough galangal and lemongrass to leave hints of Thailand flowering on one's taste buds.

"Babe, there are things called forks you know," Mark commented, his own fork halfway to his mouth as his gaze fell from her to the flowers. "What are those?" His voice was gruff and a glimpse of something dark flashed across his face.

"Pretty, don't you think?" She nodded toward the bouquet.

"Did you steal them from a neighbor's garden?"

"No, they were left at the front door." Issi spoke with a half-filled mouth.

It would have been obvious to a blind man that the revelation made him feel very uncomfortable. Mark's shoulders stiffened and the edges of his lips paled and thinned. His irises darkened to match his pupils and the hand holding his fork blanched as he tightened his grip.

A cool wariness flowed over Issi. The delicate silence which ensued, along with a tick in the corner of his eye, stopped her from confessing to him that this was the second bunch.

"It's probably just some kids. The apartments are filling up for the holidays. You remember when I got that small basket of Easter eggs in April? People are kind around here." She tried to assuage the suspicion she assumed was brewing in his mind.

His gaze darted from his food to the flowers and then to her and narrowed. "Why are you so defensive?"

"I'm not. You asked. I answered." The edge in her voice sliced the air between them - she tried to hide it with a smile, but by the way he was looking at her, she'd failed. Why was she feeling so defensive of the anonymous flower person?

"Best be wary. Can you contact the body corporate? Were there any weirdos hanging around? I think I'll try to find out who's renting here for the holidays."

"You'll do no such thing, Mark. Now calm down. One would think you'd seen ghost," she reprimanded.

At her words, Mark's face grew a shade paler and his eyes larger.

"No such things as ghosts," he mumbled. "Keep your doors locked." He picked up his fork and shoved it into his mouth before chomping and swallowing. "When will the pieces be ready for collection?"

A fine sheen of sweat erupted across his brow and his usual air of assuredness had ebbed.

"The tiger—a day. The Pratta, a few more."

"All good. I want to give the Pratta enough viewing time in the gallery before the auction. The more eyes it attracts, the more chance of you being asked for another commission." Mark picked up his phone.

Issi sighed.

Mark looked from his screen. "You know you and I make a helluva team?"

Here we go.

"I don't know why you hold back. Any man would have left ages ago. But I'm still here, babe. I love you. It's always been you, since that first day we met." He pursed his lips.

Issi turned on her chair to face him. "You know, I don't think you've ever told me how we met. Or what my work before the attack looked like. Or why we've never seen our friends in Bali again..."

"You never asked." He shifted in his seat while tugging on his tie. "Perhaps tonight. My place? I'll get the wine you like. You can wear the red number I bought you last month?" He slipped off his chair and came to stand in front of her, maneuvering himself against her crossed legs.

"I have sculptures to finish, Mark."

His fingers played with the locks that covered her left ear. "When will you let me take you to that surgeon in Thailand? He'd make you look brand-new." He tugged the curls forward.

Issi bit back her anger. "It's fine like it is. We had the best surgeon in Munich, and if he couldn't fix me, no one can."

"I didn't mean it like that, babe." Mark shrugged.

In his eyes, the sincerity of his feelings for her slithered around like eels in a barrel. But instead of quickening for him, her own emotions frightened her.

She wasn't going to play this game. Instead, she forced a smile. "We are great together when it comes to art, Mark . . ."

Mark straightened and placed both hands on her shoulders. "Look, it's not as though we need the white-picket-fence-and-children thing. I love you, Isabella; you have no one else. You can't deny our chemistry."

Issi slipped off her chair and out from under his grasp. "Have you always worn this brand of cologne?" She pressed on.

"Yes, why?"

Issi stepped away, "Just asking."

"Well your wasting my time with your ridiculous questions Issi. As you mentioned, you have work to do."

Mark looked as though he'd smelled something bad which meant he didn't like where their conversation was going.

"Didn't I have a bestie before the bomb?" She'd never thought of it before now.

There was nothing emotional to tie her to Mark and she couldn't see herself pretending any more. But now was not the time. She needed to strategize her exit of their failed relationship. It would be important to proceed in a manner that would cause the least harm to both of them. She would sit him down once both pieces were sold and when she had her money in her account. Not that she believed Mark would cheat her, but one never knew.

"You weren't exactly a social butterfly," Mark barked, then strolled into her lounge.

He had a point, if she'd had friends, wouldn't they have sought her out by now?

Issi turned and began to clear up what was left of their lunch. Mark rarely spent time at her place unless he was collecting her for an exhibition or dinner to some exotic new restaurant.

"What is this?" He pointed to her painting of the eyes and the arrow.

Shit! She'd forgotten to put it away.

"A small side project." She walked over to where he stood.

"Does it have something to do with the painting downstairs?" Mark held it up. "You never told me you were painting. This why you've taken so long with the important work, isn't it?"

"It's just my own private indulgence, Mark. Something to keep my creative juices flowing."

He placed it back down, handling it a little rougher than was appropriate, and stepped back. "You never needed to before." He stared at the work as though it were a rabid dog about to bite him. He straightened himself and turned to face her. "You sure you don't know who's leaving you those flowers?" Was that jealousy in his voice?

"Yes, Mark. I have no reason to lie about it." She placed fisted hands on her hips.

His eyes bored into her and his tongue slid across his lips as though he were tasting the truth of her words.

"Best keep it a hobby. Your painting is not near as good as your sculpting and could possibly deter potential clientele."

"As I said, it's my own personal indulgence." She tried to smile as she swallowed back her bitterness.

"Oh, before I forget, The Gallery of Modern Art contacted me. I've promised the Queensland art gallery a piece from you for their 'Flows Like Water' exhibition in

February." Mark walked back to the kitchen area and grabbed his jacket off the chair.

Issi noted that something about his usual controlled demeanor had shifted. His thoughts were elsewhere, sketching a haunted expression on his face.

"Sounds interesting. I'll think about it," she replied, keeping some distance between them.

"I've already confirmed you would." Mark pulled on his jacket and tugged on the lapels. "You have more than enough time."

"No, Mark. I said I will think about it. You're my manager, not my keeper." Issi stomped her foot, causing Mark to stop what he was doing and pin her with a look that caused her blood to rush and her muscles to tense as she moved to stand behind the chair at her kitchen bench.

His pupils enlarged as his stance softened and a smile opened up his face, but it did not reach his eyes as he walked over to where she stood.

He tugged on the lock of hair covering her ear before tracing a finger across her jaw. "I'm your fiancé. So we've hit a snag in the road; we'll get there. You need to trust that I will always know what's best for us.." He leaned forward and placed a soft kiss on her cheek. "See you later."

His eyes moved from her to the painting. A deep frown formed on his forehead. "Best you leave painting until the work is complete." The turned around and left.

What.The.Fudge!

She'd get these sculptures done and then she'd sit him down and end whatever it was he thought they could salvage. It wouldn't be easy, but it was what it was.

She needed a chai and some ocean time.

TODAY WAS HOTTER. But the sea . . . was not for swimming, except for the brave or crazy. Issi made her way along the boardwalk, sketch pad under one arm and charcoal tucked in her pocket. She took a moment to admire the large waves and the crisp blue of the horizon. Though the ocean was tumultuous, it somehow managed to retain its royal blue and streaks of turquoise.

Seductively dangerous.

Sun sprites danced beside the odd surfer atop the curl of the waves. Water was the most amazing substance. It was a force unto itself. Pliable, relaxing, devastating. Its power was unbridled, and its peace, unmatchable.

She imagined the rough currents washing away her uncomfortable morning with Mark, and focused instead on the flowers. They were disturbing in their beauty. Who the bloody hell was leaving them there?

She knew most of the people in their gated community. Several apartments were holiday rentals, and those were usually hired by families with small children.

The smell of brine warmed her insides. Who wouldn't want to wake with such beauty on their doorstep every day?

Her mind relaxed and inspiration drifted in with the hypnotic flux and wane of the tide. An image blossomed. She let go of the anger she felt toward Mark for simply okaying the job without asking her first. She'd have said yes in any case, but she was not going to stand for Mark's over-lord attitude.

A sculpture for the GOMA exhibition sketched its way into her imagination.

Not paying much attention to the world around her, Issi turned and continued her walk toward the café. In her mind's eye, shapes and angles, depths and arches, colors and features formed. Beyond the red pedestrian light there were waterways and boats. Eucalyptus trees, browns and golds, vines, and fat green grapes . . .

The here and now came rushing back when a car horn screeched as a strong arm pulled her from harm's way. Her sketch pad dropped to the ground and for the merest fraction of a second, Issi felt as though *this* was where she belonged—in this person's embrace.

"Careful now," the voice, deep and edged in gravel, warned.

Issi sensed his reluctance to let go of her. Her heart pounded like a ten-pound hammer. She spun around to come face-to-face with a blond-haired man wearing sunglasses. *Smiles and cologne guy.*

His hand slipped from the small of her back and onto her shoulder. A pair of shades blocked any expression his eyes may have proffered, but his mouth turned up and elicited the merest glimpse of a dimple on his chin. The warmth of his hand on her shoulder sent a shudder of delight along her spine as sandalwood and lavender drifted into her nose. His presence electrified the air around her.

"Oh, dear Lord. Thank you. I wasn't . . ."

His touch slid from her arm as he knelt and picked up her fallen pad, leaving Issi with the oddest sensation of abandonment.

What the heck?

"Daydreaming?" He handed her the book of drawing paper and a smile, one which burned the broken part of her mind.

"A penny for your thoughts . . ." Words she'd never uttered before fell from her lips as she tucked the block of paper beneath her right arm.

The man's Adam's apple bobbed up and down before he replied, "To be in another place."

"Far from the mundane rat race . . ." Like a waterfall after the first spring rains, words tumbled into her brain and out of her mouth. Where were they coming from? She had no idea.

"And when you least expect, visions trickle into your head . . ." he continued, shoving his hands into his pockets then pulling them out and crossing his arms across his chest.

"And so the memory slips into neglect as another comes into perspect . . ." Again, the words were there as though she'd read the poem a moment ago.

"Daydreaming . . ." they finished together.

For no reason she could fathom, tears welled in her eyes as fear, elation, and the recognizable throb of an oncoming headache fought for first place inside of Issi.

"How do you know that poem?" Issi tried to step out of the way of impatient holidaymakers who pushed past them to cross the green light, but found her limbs would not adhere to her command.

"A very special person taught it to me." He smiled, then leaned forward and took her hand before gently drawing her out of the way. The hesitation she'd perceived moments before had vanished and was now replaced with a steely confidence. The closeness of his body sent ripples of heat up and down her limbs.

Issi took a step away. She'd never experienced such a strong physical attraction and it unnerved her.

"You here on holiday?" The words rushed out her mouth before she could bite them back.

"Of sorts." He let go of her hand, walked toward the crossing and pressed the pedestrian button.

What were the chances she'd run into him the day after they'd both been to the same café?

"Are you following me?"

The stranger froze. His Adam's apple bobbed again as he wiped a hand across his mouth and his chin. "Come again?" He steadied himself as he crossed his arms.

Argh, Issi, you idiot!

"Where you staying?" She tried for a more relaxed stance but failed miserably when she discovered she didn't know what to do with her arms and hands.

"Close by." He bit his lip as a drop of perspiration trickled down his cheek.

Squeezing her drawing pad tightly between her arm and body, she slipped her hands into her pockets.

"How *close* by?"

"Up the road." He pointed in the direction of the street leading away from the ocean toward suburbia.

The traffic light turned green and the crowd that had built behind them surged forward, forcing them to cross.

"Look, can I buy you a thank-you-for-saving-me-chai or coffee, or whatever it is you drink?" He was hot, but that wasn't why she invited him. She was intrigued and she felt bad for peppering him with a gazillion questions.

His body tensed as he clenched and relaxed his hands. They came to stand on the pavement across the road. The man took a single step toward her as his mouth opened to say something before he seemed to catch himself and instead offered her a killer smile.

It tipped her insides up and over and caused her head to spin and ache.

"No thanks. I'm off to the pub. Take care now, and watch those traffic lights."

The stranger waved then made his way down the esplanade. Something odd stirred in Issi's heart. A warm sensation, like a knowing of sorts, spread through her center. The muscles in her body ached for her to run after him, but her mind balked at the idea of acting like a weirdo stalker.

What had just happened? This last week had been like one of those episodes of *The Twilight Zone* that Jeff loved to watch.

Smiles and Cologne turned the corner and disappeared, leaving her with a cold hollowness. Gone was the warm and fuzzy. She shook her head to clear her mind.

Managers, strangers, and silly flowers be damned!

5

"How was lunch with Mark?" Jeff sat as he placed a mistletoe-decorated mug of chai in front of her.

"Ugh, Mark . . . my brain . . . strangers." Issi waved her hand in front of her face. "Where do I begin?"

His large sun-tanned hand came to rest on hers. "Tell me, lovely. Jeff's always got a minute for you."

"Thanks." She prayed she wouldn't sound like she'd finally lost all her marbles. Jeff and Sam knew everything there was to know about her, which was everything she knew—but what had happened earlier sounded completely ridiculous now she thought it through. The throbbing deepened and her tongue stuck to the top of her mouth.

"So?" Jeff gave her one of his gorgeous boy-next-door grins.

"On the way down, I was daydreaming . . . I didn't see the traffic light was red and this guy, the same one from yesterday, the cologne and smile guy, pulled me to safety."

Jeff patted her hand. "So, he saved your bacon?"

"Yup, then I sprouted this poem. One I swear I've never heard or read ever, but . . . I knew it . . ." Issi leaned back and watched for signs of *call the looney bin she's lost it* to appear on her mate's face.

But all he did was rub his chin with his thumb and forefinger in consideration. "A poem?" he said and cocked his head, his gaze turning serious.

"Yeah," she answered a little too loudly, drawing the attention of the tables nearby.

Her breath caught in her throat and the world began to spin as she focused on the moment the verse had filled the empty void in her head.

Jeff moved his chair to sit beside her. "Deep. Slow. Breath. Come now. In... and out...."

Issi gripped her hands and placed them between her knees as she squeezed her legs together. Black spots blurred her vision and her lips tingled.

Jeff repeated the calming exercise with her until the world returned to a modicum of norm. Her muscles relaxed and the sensation in her lips faded.

"It's a coincidence." He reassured her.

"I've never remembered it before." She exhaled, then took a second sip of her chai.

"Remember you told Sam and me how the doctors explained new neural paths would form?" Jeff said.

"Uh-huh." She nodded.

"And that along with those new neural pathways, some old memories could return . . ." His voice faded, leaving her to follow the direction he was aiming her in.

"Like lost pieces of a puzzle. Some might match, others not so much, and anything could trigger them," she said, more to herself than her mate.

"Exactly. Do you still remember the poem?" He shifted in his seat as he leaned with his elbows on the table.

"Yes. But why now? It's been two years." Issi searched her friend's face for answers he didn't have.

"Well, I don't think neural pathways repair or grow overnight. Did the doctors give you a timeline?"

"Not exactly." She sighed and slumped in her seat. Issi took another sip and allowed the spicy sweetness to sooth her panicked insides. She placed her cup on the table and closed her eyes, then recited the poem.

"Okay. You know the poem." Jeff shrugged.

"What do you think this means?" she asked and stuck her shivering hands beneath her bum.

"I think it means you remember a poem, lovely."

"Yes, but the guy, the flowers... There were more at the front door this morning." She concentrated on keeping her voice low and her tone calm while inside she was a raging storm.

"Huh. A secret admirer?"

"Who, Jeff? It's only you, Sam, and Mark. I have no other friends. I only know my neighbors by sight—so who can it be?"

"Well, perhaps it's a holiday rental? Remember Easter when that kid delivered chocolate bunnies to all the residents? And, oh boy, last Christmas, how many fruitcakes were left at your door?"

"Too many," Issi grumbled.

She hated fruitcake, but had loved the gesture and ended up sculpting every resident a Christmas tree decoration as thanks.

"See? You live among some real friendly people." Jeff tried to assure her.

"Yeah, but do you think everyone's getting flowers every morning? Or is there some weird, crazy person who's trying to freak me out?"

Jeff gripped her hand in his. "I don't know, but my gut is telling me we shouldn't jump to conclusions again. Remember the vineyard last month? You were convinced you had some connection to the place because something about it smelled familiar? But it was simply a bit of memory, a lost piece of recognition your brain wasn't sure what to do with. Your filing cabinet has been ripped apart and all you're left with are bits of the past that have no home—make sense?"

"Yes. But it's as though it's all happening at once." She threw her hands up and allowed them to fall into her lap.

"Exactly. Look, my dear, you're living with a condition which literally affects one in a couple of hundred thousand people. For you, I would dare to say that this might be normal. You were told things like this could happen. Your memory could come back in bits and pieces, or in chunks—like a jigsaw puzzle. That your subconscious would continually grasp at things and try to make connections. Those pieces could eventually fit together to give you a full picture."

"Or they could just remain lost fragments of nothing." She swallowed the tears that threatened mutiny. She was not going to dissolve into a blubbering mess.

Jeff sighed. "Yup. So, how's 'bout we take it one memory at a time? Go look the poem up later. I've not heard it before, but then, I don't read poetry. Maybe you used to?"

Issi reached across and hugged him. "Thanks. I don't know what I'd do without you guys."

"And what would we do without our lovely Isabella?" Jeff stood and patted her shoulder. "Sit and enjoy the view."

Issi stared out across the esplanade at the ocean. Jeff had a point. The mystery bloke was probably a sheer coincidence, but the poem . . . She made a mental note to do some research when she had a moment to spare.

Some part of her niggled and wouldn't settle down. This wasn't a smell or a sense of déjà vu. It was a poem and flowers, a painting and a pair of eyes which haunted her. A sense of knowing, but not seeing. One which had stirred a hurricane deep within her. She took another deep breath. Too many odd things happening at once. Was she paranoid?

Some sculpting would help soothe her frantic mind. Perhaps if she put the ideas which had blossomed on the way down on paper, she'd be able to distract herself long enough to be able to make sense of it all later.

Jeff called out from the counter. "Lovely, wanna try some of Sam's new raspberry curd tart with shortbread crust?"

"Yes please!" She nodded.

"Are you game to try my Santa's Sleigh Bells mocktail with it?" Jeff's eyes twinkled as a cheeky grin spread across his face.

"Oh, why not." Issi laughed.

If the guys kept on using her as their guinea pig for new recipes, she'd be rolling around the bustling seaside soon.

An electric flutter of ethereal fingers stroked the back of her neck. Issi took a break from her sketching, her eyes grazed across the tables, and patrons, then focused on passers-by. The feeling she was being watched waded into her consciousness. *Argh, enough!* This was all too much. Seriously, she was her own worst enemy.

She rolled her head left to right to let go of the tension eating at her shoulders and neck muscles.

No more thinking—just being. She inhaled deeply, held her breath for five counts, and let it go and focused on her sketch. As her hand deftly flowed across the page, guiding the charcoal this way and that, an image came to life in black strokes she shaded on the white block of paper.

Once she was happy with her draft, Issi closed her drawing pad.

She simply had to make peace with the fact that days like today were a part of who she now was.

Her gaze followed the roll and crash of turquoise water onto the holidaymaker-dotted sand.

Her artist's mind dwelled on the colors of the busy landscape before her. Thank goodness she'd not lost her ability to create. A person's memory was bad enough, but without her art, she'd be a hollow windblown husk.

———

THE COOL DESCENT of dusk greeted Issi as she walked through her front door. She'd spent her afternoon eating and chilling on the deck of Jeff and Sam's café.

The guys had used her prolonged presence to test out new mocktails and the odd cocktail they'd concocted to attract the holiday crowd. Her favorite so far was their 'Christmas Tree.' It was a mixture of vodka and lemonade with streaks of green, red, and bright yellow liquors twirled through the drink to give the impression of a decorated tree. While she could only manage one of those, it'd be a winner and certainly broke a person's thirst.

They'd also been kind enough to drop her off on their way home.

The void in her mind echoed off the empty walls of her apartment.

Perhaps it was time for a change.

Issi dropped her phone and keys on the kitchen counter and made her way downstairs to her studio where she grabbed a few nails she had from a tool box and shoved them into her pants pocket. With the hammer clenched in one hand, she carefully lifted the painting she'd procured at the market off the easel. Trying not to trip over her feet, she stumbled back to her living room.

Resting it against the wall, she took off her shoes, dug out a nail and grabbed the hammer. Standing on the couch, she positioned the nail and made a mark on the wall, then stepped down and tried to imagine the painting hanging there to judge if the height was correct. Eventually Issi simply hammered away, hoping she'd hit a balk and missed anything electrical or water-laden, such as a pipe. She could have called the guys to help her, but she wanted to do this now.

Thankfully she didn't have to answer to a landlord if she stuffed up. She'd bought the apartment soon after moving to the Sunshine Coast with Mark, instinctively knowing she needed her own space.

By some form of luck, the nail held, the lights still worked, and there was no water pouring through the gyprock.

Hammer in one hand and sweat dripping off her forehead, Issi stood back and admired the forty-eight-by-sixty-inch canvas.

The painting was of a vineyard in a place called Constantia, the South African woman had said, and was simply breathtaking. The artist had experienced a sad, lonely life and a violent end, according to that short blurb Jeff had managed to dig up on the internet. The hair on her arms stood at attention as she read the signature—*Van Rooyen*—in the bottom left-hand corner.

Issi ignored the unsettling sensation and focused on the comfort the painting brought to her home.

She laid the hammer on the floor then brought her hands together beneath her chin. The portrait reached out to her from its acrylic world. The sky, the grapes, the cool damp soil all called to her.

The artwork filled her with joy.

Her phone vibrated.

Babe, I'll pick you up for dinner?

The message doused her enthusiasm. She didn't need to think about her answer. A small wave of guilt washed over her, but she wasn't in the frame of mind to sort out her relationship now.

Her thumb tapped the screen.

Working on the Pratta.

A little white lie—the sculpture could wait until morning. She tucked her phone away, ignoring his reply.

She turned her attention to the other canvas in her lounge. The one she'd created and had Mark in a twist.

She should take it back to her studio—it wasn't finished.

As carefully as she had brought the other painting up, she returned hers to the safety of her studio.

Issi placed it on the easel she'd removed the landscape from and stared at the hazel eyes. Lines and contours began to form in her mind.

With charcoal gripped between eager fingers, her hand moved this way and that. And soon a profile came to life. It wasn't complete; like in her memories, it was fragmented. A jawline here and a cheek bone there. Where had she seen this face before?

Her hand continued to move as though it had a life of its own. Lines turned into shapes and shapes into shadows. When her fingers, elbow, and biceps felt like they could move no more, she stepped away and took a deep breath. Her head twirled as she sucked in a mouthful of warm air.

Was she drawing inspiration from the familiar? Had cologne-and-smiles man made such an impression on her brain that she'd simply reached for a face to match the eyes that stared back from an incomplete sketch? She could complete the entire profile by simply drawing on her memory of him. Was her memory simply reaching for anything to fill the void? What was she missing?

Exhaustion set in.

Issi reached for the eyes. Her index finger traced the soft lines of the lower lids.

A chill washed over her. She rubbed her hands up and down her arms to ward off the eerie sensation. *God!* She was losing her mind.

Remember!

What was her brain trying to tell her? Which dots was she failing to connect?

"Perhaps it's because there are no dots to connect, you silly girl," she chastised herself.

A jab behind her eye and a tangy metallic taste in her mouth told her she'd overdone it. Headaches and migraines were part and parcel of Issi after the bombing. Especially on the days when she did too much.

She closed and locked the balcony doors, switched off all her lights, which always intensified the throbbing, and made her way to the bathroom.

Then felt around on the second shelf of the cupboard beneath the bathroom sink. Her hand landed on a cardboard box the size of a pack of Smarties. A chemical cocktail to help curb the cracking pain headed her way. She popped the pills from her hand into her mouth, then filled the glass at her basin with water and washed them down. Replacing the box, she grabbed a pill container. She tucked the single tablet into her pocket.

Issi grabbed a pillow and the air-conditioning remote off her bedside table and lay on the cool wood of her bedroom floor. She placed her glass of water beside the pillow. Lifting her right hand, she aimed the small square remote at the unit above her bed and pressed the power button. Cool air rushed through the room, and she allowed herself to relax.

What would her life have been like if not for the bomb? She would never have met Jeff or Sam. But would she have still been in love with Mark? They probably would have been married by now. Issi shuddered again—she couldn't believe it would have been a happy marriage.

As far as she could figure out, she'd had no one but Mark back in WA. Her parents had both passed away a few years earlier and she'd not seen any of their friends since their return from Munich. So, as cruel as it was to think of, perhaps fate's hand had dealt her a semi-good one, even if it had been at a cost. But why, why in the world did she still feel so very alone? As though the center of her universe were missing and her life spun on an axis-less plane?

In Munich, most of the survivors had been admitted to the same hospital after the bomb decimated an entire boarding gate. The hospital had one of the best burn and neurological units in the country.

Her wounds were nothing compared to some. Only the side of her head and neck had been injured. Granted they were worse than your average knee-scrape, but still, she'd come off lightly. Her right hand instinctively touched the taut bumpy flesh that had once been her ear. It was mostly the damage to her skull and brain which had concerned the doctors.

It had taken her six weeks before her hearing had returned. It took another month to discern sounds and see color. Weird how the brain worked; had it altered her art as well? Because of the house fire, there was none of her past work to compare with her recent art and no way of knowing if she'd liked painting as much as she did now. She'd asked Mark if any were on her Instagram page, but he'd explained that away too. Something about deleting the past and only posting her latest and greatest.

After returning, everything had been a whirlwind. She'd trusted Mark and never once thought about life beyond the bubble she'd built around herself. Mark had never been comfortable discussing too much about their lives before the bombing, except when it was to try and encourage her to be more intimate with him.

It was just before she'd been released from hospital that her fingertips begged for her to create something. She hadn't had paper so she'd asked a nurse if she could borrow a pencil and sketched the image on a serviette. It was only then that Mark told her about her spectacular gift.

Another sharp stab sliced the area behind her eyes.

Issi sat slowly and sipped her water, then leaned forward with her head resting between her knees.

She remembered nothing of that fateful day except for the odd flash of bright light and something hard and hot knocking her down. She'd awoken three days after they'd pulled her out of an induced coma.

The pounding in her skull picked up pace and bile burned the back of her throat. Issi lay back. She hoped the concoction would put her to sleep before the full-on thumping commenced. She reached into her pocket where she'd put a tablet—a morphine derivative. Only to be used if the concoction failed.

Half an hour later, a tirade of bouncing kangaroos thrummed their way around the inside of her skull. With care, she crawled back to her pillow from the bathroom.

Nausea and vomiting often accompanied the bouts of headaches.

She fiddled with the round tablet. She hated the effects morphine had on her, but it was either that or a nauseating hammering for the next few hours. Issi rolled on to her side, pushed up with her elbow and pulled the tablet from her pant pocket.

Sleep. I just need to sleep.

6

THE TWO MEN FROM FRED AND SONS COURIERS WRAPPED THE
Pratta with the care of a mother laying down her newborn
babe. They then turned their attentions to the second
sculpture.

"Why are you packing my tiger into that crate? It seems
far too big to keep it steady and safe," Issi slipped off her
chair as they lifted the heavily bubble and rice paper-
wrapped art work.

"Er, it was the instructions given to us." The man
glanced at her, looking somewhat offended. "Take it up with
your manger. He booked the transportation as he always
does."

Issi sighed and hoped Mark knew what he was doing—
normally she would have called him about an issue like this,
but she'd taken a week instead of the two days she'd
promised to finish both pieces and Mark was not a happy
man. Her headache had taken longer to clear, and the
effects of the medication had left her dull and useless
afterward.

"If you'd sign here." The older man handed her a clipboard.

She took it and scribbled her name on the allotted line.

Once the men left through the bottom studio door, she made her way upstairs to the kitchen. She grabbed a glass out of the cupboard and filled it with ice-cold water. Her thirst always lingered after a bad headache—a side-effect of the medication.

She refilled the glass and returned to her balcony where she plonked onto a chair. There'd be no creating today. She needed to take a step back; to wait for the last of the medication to work out of her system before she put down any more ideas for her GOMA sculpture.

Issi sighed gratefully as she took in the picturesque scene before her—she was blessed. While she didn't have the strength to create, she didn't feel like sitting here doing nothing either. Perhaps now would be a good time to look up the poem? She had planned to days ago, but with her migraine and finishing the sculptures, she'd not had time.

Putting down her glass, she stood and retrieved her iPad from inside then returned to her seat at her outdoor table.

It was another scorcher of a day. The sea had calmed—so had the breeze. The outside fan brought little relief from the cloying humidity. Perhaps she'd go for a swim later this afternoon.

She tapped the screen. 'Poetry'. No, that wouldn't do. She deleted the word from the search box, then typed in 'English Poetry—Daydreaming.'

Names and poems popped open on the screen. None of them titled *Daydreaming*. Nonetheless, Issi soaked up all there was on offer. Like a child who'd only recently learned to read, Issi found she liked poetry quite a bit. The rhythm and the words called to her.

Old poems, new poems, silly poems. Words that brought tears to her eyes and painted worlds filled with love, glory, treachery, and death. Astonishingly, some she knew off by heart and others seemed vaguely familiar.

Had she always loved poetry? Wouldn't this be something that Mark would've known about her? Issi wanted to jump for joy. She had discovered something new about her old-self and it was exhilarating!

She. Loved. Poetry.

Her heart throbbed and her nerves froze when she happened on a poem based on an ancient legend.

It told of a forbidden and deep love between a warrior and a princess. Issi stared at the screen until the words began to swim.

This had meant something to her once. The weight of the verses familiarity clung to her heart.

Her phone gave off a shrill squawk and she jumped, knocking over her glass of water—Mark.

"Babe, the sculptures have just arrived. Congratulations! I'm going to take you out to celebrate tonight."

"Mark, you won't believe this . . ." She had to share her news with someone.

"You've started on your next piece? You're a machine, babe, an absolute creative machine!"

"Uh, no . . . I've had a breakthrough."

"A breakthrough? You mean with your sculpture for the GOMA?"

"No! Mark, I remembered . . . I think . . . I loved, well, love poetry! Isn't this great? Why didn't you tell me I enjoyed it so much?"

Silence.

"Mark, you there?"

"Yes. Not near as important as the GOMA. Look, just be

ready at seven. I'll book a table at The Bistro in Noosa. Babe
. . . it's all about us tonight, so wear something hot, okay?"

Issi held the phone away from her face and glared at the
screen. She tapped the red icon.

To hell with you Mark Cornwall.

She was sick and tired of his bullshit attitude. Why had
he ignored her question? Was it that he was more excited
about her sculptures and less so about her discovering
something about herself? Or was there more to it?

He'd simply slapped the fact she'd remembered a vital
part of herself down as though it were an irritating insect. If
he truly cared about her the way he so often made out, he'd
have given a damn. He'd have told her about her penchant
for poetry. What else was he hiding from her? Her thoughts
returned to the afternoon he'd seen her painting.

After opening the messaging app on her phone, Issi
typed a text to Mark. *We need to chat. Meet me at Poet's Café in
Peregian Beach at six pm.*

Her head still buzzed from the painkillers, it was time
for a swim. Nothing like mother nature's elixir to wash away
her anger and help her see the path she'd chosen to follow,
with more clarity. It was time to end things with Mark, but
not before she got answers. There was no doubt in her
mind, he was hiding something from her.

———

ISSI DROPPED her towel on the ground. The soles of her feet
stung as they touched the sunbaked sand. She walked to the
edge of the water and allowed the waves to trickle over her
toes.

Oh, the water is amazing.

Wet coolness soaked her feet and splashed against her ankles, soothing compared to the heat of the day.

She waded in until she was waist-deep, her breath hitching in her throat as the briny liquid tickled her torso. Before she lost her nerve, Issi dove beneath the waves. It rolled over her body like the practiced fingers of a masseuse. She swam until she was behind the breakers, then twisted onto her back and floated. The sea lapped her thighs and face, and the sun bit at her skin.

Mark was an ass. Only her art and how much he could make out of it mattered to him—well, that and getting her into his bed. As for their 'relationship,' there hadn't been one since she'd regained consciousness, and it was clear there never would be.

Surely she could find another manager? She wouldn't ignore the ice in his tone when she'd told him of the poetry. She was certain there was more to it, but she simply couldn't put her finger on it.

A cold feeling crept into the hollows of her heart as she floated in the comforting waters. She didn't believe Mark would let her go that easily.

It wasn't going to be as simple as sitting him down and getting her answers. Something told her that attempt would be as futile as looking for a new manager.

A freak wave roared as it rolled up and crashed into her. It pushed her into a sandbank below the surface. She gasped, but there was no air to be found as water rushed into her mouth and drenched her lungs. Panic surged through her limbs as she kicked and swatted at the water around her. The instinctive need to open her mouth and gasp for air fought her better judgement.

Het feet touched a sandbank and she kicked hard at the

same time as she reached up and pushed down hard with her arms.

Issi broke through the surface with splutter. Wiping salt and sand from her eyes, she forced them open. *Shit!* She was in a rip. Before she could decide on a plan of action, another wave came crashing on top of her as the current pulled her farther out.

She flailed and choked. The water burned her eyes and the surf knocked her about. Issi kicked and paddled as best she could. The inside of her chest burned and her legs and arms ached.

Exhausted and petrified, she managed to break the surface once more but not for long as another wave dunked her. With no strength left, she stopped fighting as her body began to drift, down, down . . . The salty water dimmed her vision and the sun's rays grew duller the deeper she sank.

Flashes of life awoke inside her head. A vineyard and a brownstone building. Hazel eyes and the warm kiss of a lover. An arrow with a red tail, aimed at her heart. Darkness and release. This was it. She'd survived a terrorist attack only to drown in her beloved ocean.

A strong arm wrapped itself around her waist and pulled her upwards.

As her head broke the surface, instinct took over and she drew in the mouthful of air. Her lungs bubbled and cracked as they fought to absorb air and not water.

"Shhh, Issi. Lie back. I've got you."

The words, like a magic spell, brought instant calm.

That voice—strong and edged with a gravely base. She relished the tight grip which snaked around her midriff.

Exhausted, she gave in and leaned into the chest of her rescuer. Ripped muscles pushed into her back as he swam them to shore. Waves washed over them and the sun blurred her vision.

"Who are you?" she croaked.

"Who are you, Issi?"

"I'm me." Her words slurred as she tried to process his question and her odd response. Why was he calling her Issi?

They reached the shore and the strong arm holding her close shifted as the other slid beneath her legs. Her head still spun from being dunked and battered by the ocean, but she couldn't help feeling these arms would keep her safe. The sun blinded her and she was unable to make out his face. But it was him. The stranger from the other day. She just knew it.

"God! Is she okay?" Concern soaked the woman's voice. "I called for an ambulance. Dear, are you okay? I'm a nurse. Here, let me help you onto your side."

The man lowered Issi onto a towel. His strong arms slipped away, leaving her feeling cold and alone as the woman began to fuss over her.

"Who are you?" Issi spluttered.

"I need you to . . ."

"Do you know this man?" the woman's voice cut the stranger's reply in half.

"N-no, but . . ."

"Probably best you give her some room." The nurse ordered.

"W-wait!" she called out, then coughed. Saltwater worked its way along her throat and she had to twist her head as her stomach expelled half the ocean.

———

"BABE, good God, what were you thinking?" Mark said as he approached the trolley where she lay with an oxygen mask covering her face.

Issi glared at him over the rim of the mask. She was still upset with him. She was upset with herself, and she was incredibly upset with the man who'd saved her life a second time and simply vanished in the wind.

"Are you family?" the paramedic asked.

"Yes," Mark blurted.

Issi wanted to set him straight, but the paramedics swiftly pushed the trolley into the back of the ambulance before instructing Mark to follow them to the hospital.

———

MARK NAVIGATED the car along her street. "I didn't appreciate you hanging up on me like that, but perhaps on a day like today it worked out for the best, eh? Who knows what could have happened had I not come looking for you when I did?"

"Didn't you get my text?" She instinctively reached for her handbag then remembered she'd been rushed off to hospital in only her bathers and now sat wrapped in a towel on the front seat of Mark's car.

Mark shook his head.

He was lying; she could tell.

Issi bit back her frustration and said nothing.

"Look, babe, I honestly think it's best you pack a bag and spend the weekend with me."

Issi shifted on the seat of his swank Mercedes-Benz. "Just give me a moment to gather myself, Mark."

Why didn't she say no? She was a silly woman, dragging out the inevitable. But her thoughts felt foggy following the afternoon's near-drowning and she was too tired to attempt that conversation with Mark right now. It'd have to wait, but not for long.

Mark pulled up to the gate of her complex. Thankfully, the nurse who had stayed by her after her cologne and smiles man had taken off, had had the foresight to make sure her keys and towel accompanied her to the hospital.

Issi reached forward and pressed the remote which opened the gate. Mark drove in, slower than usual. Goose bumps broke out all over her body as she noticed the sharp attention Mark paid to his surroundings.

"Looking for something?" She glanced in the direction he was squinting.

"Just making sure no children run out in front of me. Parents really should watch them." He parked outside her apartment.

Issi shook her head. He'd never worried about wayward kids before.

She stumbled out of the car as he strolled around and snuck an arm around her, which she quickly shrugged off. At the door, she slipped a key into the lock.

"I want to leave in five minutes," Mark barked.

Issi swallowed the urge to scream, *just fuck off!*

Instead, she flung open the screen door then unlocked her front door and pushed it open.

She'd left her phone on the kitchen counter that afternoon. The screen glowed an impatient green. Twenty missed calls and double the messages. *Shit!*

"Did you let the guys know what had happened like I asked you to?"

"Yes. But I told them I'd handle it," Mark blurted angrily.

She grabbed the phone and tapped her speed dial.

"Are you okay? Fuck's sake, Isabella . . . " Jeff's frantic barrage added to her guilt.

"I'm okay. Sorry. I left my phone at home. I'm okay. Mark's brought me home."

"Yeah we know. That's what the nurse at the hospital told us." Issi didn't miss the anger in his tone.

"You came to the hospital?" She turned to face Mark who shot her an innocent glance.

"Yeah, but you'd already been discharged."

"Oh." Issi let out a huff as she pulled her fingers through her sea-knotted tresses. "We're home now."

"Sam and I are on our way."

She put the phone down and a sense of relief snuck into her heart. She didn't want to go anywhere with Mark and he wasn't going to take no for an answer.

"Why is it you put in more time and effort with your hippie friends from the café than you do with us?" Mark asked as he searched her fridge. "Don't you have other wine beside Moscato?"

Issi didn't have the strength and simply ignored his question.

"I want you to pack a bag and come home with me," he ordered as he poured himself a glass and drank.

She sat at the counter and rested her head on her hands. She needed peace and quiet. She needed to go over what had happened that afternoon, and she had to figure out why the stranger always seemed to be there at the right moment. Her gut told her it was no coincidence and the realization gripped her insides like a vise.

Another memory slipped into place, not from her past, but from that afternoon. The stranger had called her Issi. No one called her Issi except herself. She glanced over at the flowers.

"Babe, are you listening to me?" Mark asked.

"What?" She raised her head.

"Pack your bag. You're in no condition to stay alone after what you've been through."

"I'm staying here, Mark. In my own home." Issi leaned back in the chair.

Mark stood opposite her, wine glass in one hand, scowling, as the fingers of his other hand rapped an annoying tattoo on the counter. He took a deep sip then placed his glass down.

A ripple of fear ran over her skin as he considered her with his darkening gaze. The tip of his tongue ran along his top lip. He walked around and came to stand where she sat.

"You are the most beautiful creature I have ever laid my eyes on, Isabella. You are talented and independent, but you are also mine. I patiently nurtured you. Without me you'd not be the brilliant, successful, artist you are." His use of the word set all sorts of alarm bells off and her blood ran cold. Mark Cornwall was a hell of a lot more than an arrogant, controlling yuppie.

He was dangerous and he wasn't going to let her go without a fight.

Issi gripped the seat of the chair at the kitchen counter as she sprinted through a myriad of exit strategies when a cold thought slithered across her mind. "How did you know where to find me this afternoon?"

Placing both hands on her upper arms, his expression hardened as did his grip. His eyes turned to coal and his lips thinned. "Isabella, darling...I always know where to find you. Now go pack your bags, we're leaving."

7

A SUDDEN, LOUD BANG ECHOED THROUGH THE APARTMENT AS fists beat against her front door.

"It's open." A wave of absolute relief washed over her. The guys had arrived.

Jeff and Sam rushed into her apartment and straight to her. Mark had to step back as the pair pushed past and wrapped their arms around her.

"Thank God you're okay!" Sam drew her into his strong arms.

"Okay, guys, no need to crowd her," Mark interjected.

Ignoring him, Jeff stepped closer as Sam turned, hanging his arm protectively around her shoulders. Mark was a sturdy unit, but he was no match for her mates who were both taller and bulkier than him.

"What happened, lovely? The first we heard of it was Mark phoning us." Sam looked at Mark.

His gaze narrowed as he took aim with his words. "Thanks for that, by the way."

She squeezed her arms around the guys. "Sorry," was all she could offer.

"She's just fine, thank you, and about to pack her bags and come home with me." Mark almost spat the words from across the counter.

Jeff looked at her, eyebrow arched. "It's probably better you're not alone tonight?"

"Yes." But it wouldn't be in Mark's company, that was for sure.

With a deadpan glare aimed at Mark, Jeff said, "It's okay, mate. We'll stay." Then looking back at her, he added, "Are you okay with that?"

"Of course." Issi nodded, trying not to look too relieved.

A defeated Mark's cheeks flushed and his chest rose and fell. "I'll call in the morning."

Sam closed the door the moment Mark exited. "Why do I get the feeling we arrived in time?"

Issi rubbed her hands over her face. "I need a shower and then a glass of wine, *and then* I'll tell you all about it."

———

"So, WHAT HAPPENED?" Jeff placed the stacked boxes of pizza down on her coffee table beside the serviettes and plates.

They huddled on her couch, the air conditioner pumping out a cooler breeze than the one sweeping up from the ocean on her balcony.

Issi cupped her glass of Moscato. Where to begin? She pulled her fingers through her hair, not caring if the guys saw her scars. "When the water dragged me down... I thought, *this is it.*"

"Oh lovely." Sam shifted on his seat and reached out to place a comforting hand on her knee.

Issi sat upright and inhaled deeply before coughing. Her chest still hurt and her lungs burned a little. The doctor at the emergency department had told her to remain vigilant, and that if anything felt wrong to come right back in. He'd warned her of the possibility of secondary drowning. With a slice of meatlovers in one hand and her wine in the other, Issi wove her colorful tale of nearly drowning and dramatic rescue.

"He? Mark saved you?" Sam's voice rose an octave.

"No. The guy from the coffee shop – cologne and smiles." Issi huffed and dropped the crust on her plate. Standing she stretched her arms out above her head. Her body would feel every punch and dump the ocean had given her tomorrow, that was for sure. She strolled toward the glass doors and slid them apart.

The sun had set and the ocean lay like a blanket of ink spreading out toward an endless horizon. A soft, gravelly voice tripped across her memory. *Who are you, Issi?*

Jeff came to stand beside her. "So he happened to be out swimming the same time as you? "

Issi glanced at her friend. It sounded out-of-this-world crazy, but . . . "Yes, I suppose it's possible. But that's not what was weird."

"You obviously have a different definition for weird my dear." Sam joined them placing their glasses and the bottle on the glass table top.

"He asked me if I knew who I was?" Issi reached for her wine, swallowed a mouthful, then wiped her mouth with the back of her hand.

"Slow down there, love." Jeff reached forward and poured her a little more.

"I need to show you both something. Wait here. I'll be back." She took off toward her studio. The painting of the eyes. It was a long shot, but Issi wondered if it had anything to do with everything else that was happening.

She returned and leaned it against the balcony railing, and the three of them sat in contemplative silence.

It was Sam who spoke first. "You've added facial features."

Jeff rubbed his chin. "I've seen this before . . . Issi, the other sketch on the canvas—the face with the shades!"

His words rocked her.

"Can you remember any more of it?"

"The face?" She folded her arms. It wasn't cold but a chill had settled inside of her.

"Yeah. Is it a face drawn from memory or..." Jeff cocked his head.

"That's my greatest conundrum." Issi stepped back from the painting and considered Jeff's question. "When I was halfway through "—she pointed a shaking finger to the portrait, "I realized I knew the face."

Issi sighed, sat on one of the chairs, lifted her legs off the floor and folded them against her, focusing on the half-sketched face.

"Well, don't leave us hanging." Sam sat in the chair beside her placing his arms on the table when she didn't finish.

"It's his. Cologne and Smiles' face. I thought I was reaching, that my mind wanted to give the eyes a face, but now . . ."

"And those are *his* eyes?" Jeff pointed, flabbergasted, to the canvas.

"I've not seen them." Issi stared at her canvas. Her tears returned. She fought them back but a few escaped and ran down her cheek.

"Oh, lovely. It's gonna be okay." Jeff shifted his chair until he came to sit beside her with his arm reaching around her.

"So much has happened in the last weeks. I can't keep

up." She sniffed and used her T-shirt as a tissue. "I mean, for months I've been searching and when I finally think I've gotten to a point where I can make peace with my lost past —wham! All this happens."

"Has Mark seen this?" Sam asked.

"Yes. He hates it. Told me to stop painting."

The guys gave her shocked glances.

"What?" Sam exclaimed. "What's Mark on about, and why did you look so relieved when he left?"

Issi's mouth dried, and she swallowed hard as she wiped away the last of her tears. "He's been pushing me for more. He wants us to be what we were before the bomb. But I can't. And when I put my foot down this evening he got really weird—as in, *scary psycho* weird."

"Oh no, lovely. You need to kick this buffalo in the butt and quick." Jeff squeezed her shoulder then let go.

"I don't think he's the kind of guy who takes no for an answer." She rubbed her hands together, then pushed them under her butt.

"You'll have to be straight with him at some point. You can't leave it to sort itself out anymore. Jeff and I will arrange that one or both of us will be with you when you're ready to face him."

"Oh, guys, that's not necessary—"

Her mate placed a hand on her shoulder. "Of course it is. Until you are able to source a new manager, we'll help you deal with business."

"Yeah, and I wonder if we shouldn't try figure out who Mr. Cologne and Smiles is while we're at it?" Sam added.

Issi stared at the half-finished panting. A change was coming; she could feel it. The only thing she could do was hope it was all for the best.

Issi settled her mates into her bedroom for the night.

"I'll be fine out here," she explained when they tried to argue.

She dropped her pillow and a doona on the floor of her living room, then walked out onto the verandah.

The weather had taken a sudden turn. The breeze had morphed into a gust, whipping sea spray off the waves. Angry fists billowed across the horizon as jagged white streaks lit up the night. A low grumbling echoed across a volatile ocean, echoing her inner frustration. Rain would bring some much-needed relief to the dry summer the south-east coast was experiencing. She leaned on the railing and peered down at the water which had so very nearly stolen her life that afternoon.

Who are you, Issi?

She gasped and took a step back. The words were as clear as though someone had stood behind her and whispered them into her ears.

The mind was a wicked thing. Who was this man? Did she want to know? She'd read of people being stalked, but was this what that was?

Too much.

Issi sunk to the floor and let go of the reins on her emotions. Frustrated tears burst their banks as she wept into her hands. Fear scoured its way across her chest in waves of fiery anger that clawed at the muscles in her throat.

Pushing her face into her knees, Issi allowed the cathartic sensation to override her need for composure and strength.

Why was Mark acting like a such a brute? The way he'd

behaved this afternoon, him making it clear he saw her as his, scared the crap out of her. What was he hiding?

And the stranger who'd saved her? Why had he been there? It was far more than coincidence, but still, it was bordering on creepy. And then there was the near-drowning.

Issi allowed the fear of dying and the grief of losing something she couldn't even remember wash over her as a fresh wave of tears took hold. There were too many unanswered questions and even more weird coincidences for any sane human to make sense of, let alone a woman with no past and a broken brain.

Once her sobbing calmed, she stood and inhaled the wild ocean air. The breeze dried her tears but refused to carry the heaviness in her heart away with it.

Who are you, Issi?

"Bugger off!" she shouted out across the dark of night.

8

"YOU'D MENTIONED YOU PREFERRED THE FLOOR, BUT I NEVER imagined you were serious."

Issi awoke to find Jeff standing over her with a steaming cup of awesome in his hand. She pushed herself upward with one arm and rubbed the sleep and fog from her eyes with her other.

"The open doors make me feel less trapped." She stood and took the mug from her friend.

"Well, we're off." He glanced back as Sam strolled out from the bedroom.

"We need to stop home first and get some fresh clothes for the day." Sam, who was dressed in a crinkled shirt and yesterday's surf shorts, stretched his long arms and yawned.

"You both sleep okay?" She smiled over the rim of her steaming mug.

"Yup. But next time try not to yell at the ocean. You gave me a heart attack," Jeff shook his head as he rinsed his mug at the basin.

"Sorry. I was pissed." Issi proffered a shy smile.

"No shit." Sam winked. "Come on, slow poke. Work waits for no one."

"Chat later, lovely." Jeff leaned forward and placed a kiss on her forehead. "Now remember, no alone time with Mark. My phone's on vibrate in my pocket. And you're sure he has no access to your apartment?"

"Yes, sir, captain, sir. And nope." She play-saluted her friends as they stepped out the front door.

Issi locked it behind them then finished her coffee and stared at the painting standing on the floor. Perhaps it didn't need to be finished, but only wanted some color? So what if the face resembled Cologne and Smiles?

A few moments later, she trotted up the stairs of her studio, easel under one arm and paints and brushes in the other.

With her palette in one hand, she dabbed her brush into the vibrant sanguine paint then brushed it across the jawline. Her inspiration called for out-of-the-box instead of the expected. Her strokes were solid and defined, ending with a lighter touch. They gave the impression she wanted. She blended her colors until there was no longer any charcoal visible. Blues instead of black, yellow instead of beige—the canvas came to life.

The motion of painting and mixing colors was hypnotic. When sculpting, Issi found she vanished into a world of texture, shades, and shapes. But with painting, she was riding a magic carpet across the stars. She stepped back and allowed her memories of the day she'd exchanged lines of a poem with the stranger to surface. Her heart gave a thud as a plethora of butterflies swirled around her insides. Who was the man and why did the mere thought of him send her heart and her mind into an almighty frenzy?

Issi shifted her gaze from the portrait to the ocean. Last

night had brought on an almighty wind and lightning storm, but no rain. It was another steamy hot Queensland day. She turned the easel just so and considered her work.

The natural light complemented her painting and eccentric use of color. Her heart swelled with joy, then stuttered. She needed some fresh air.

Issi cleaned up her paints and brushes. *Time for a walk.*

Something had shifted after her crying session last night. While she still wanted answers, her soul felt lighter, almost buoyant.

Slipping on a pair of thongs, Issi grabbed her phone and keys. She'd missed a text from Mark. *We need to talk please. I know I came across a little demanding yesterday, but it's because I was worried. Babe, I love you!! I am on my way over to discuss our options.*

Oh no he wasn't!

I'm out. Was all she texted. His message screamed desperation, and some part of her knew that in a man like Mark, that was dangerous. She'd set the time and the place. And then she'd break it off on her terms.

Issi closed her phone and tucked it into the back pocket of her khaki shorts.

It was time to exorcise these pesky demons. She flung open her front door and then the gate, almost stepping on the bunch of flowers laying on her welcome mat.

Who are you, Issi?

Her heart thumped harder and her stomach flick-flacked.

She knelt and picked up the pretty blooms.

'Who are you!' She shouted then ducked inside when her neighbor gave her a odd glance from where she stood watering her hydrangea's. She fled back inside, paused beside her kitchen counter, then summarily dumped them in the bin. Something had to give—things could not go on like this.

Issi peeked out the window. Her neighbor had vanished. She stepped outside, making sure to lock her door and gate behind her.

Trotting down the steps she came to stand on the paved driveway. Hands on hips, she gave the apartments a thorough once-over, or as good an inspection as she could from where she stood.

The thought that Cologne and Smiles guy possibly lived in the complex and was the flower deliverer was not lost on her, and sent an uncomfortable chill down her spine for the first time.

When she returned from her walk, she was going to google a private investigator.

She needed to find out who this man was. But first, some soul food was in order. Sighing, Issi made her way to the easterly gate leading to the boardwalk and Point Arkwright Beach.

She unlocked the gate and stepped out onto the side of the road, before crossing it and coming to stand on the boardwalk. The humidity covered everyone and everything in a layer of divine summer stickiness. The ocean rolled and receded inviting her to come in and cool down. Her skin erupted in gooseflesh at the memory of her near drowning.

Issi, who are you?

She mulled over the words whispered into her ear the day before. The damn words would simply not let her be. What did this man know about her that she could not remember and what invisible cord was his question plucking on?

She'd always sensed she was more than Mark told her she'd been, but healing from the trauma she'd survived after the bombing had taken up so much of her energy. She'd mentally mopped herself into a corner of safety.

Should she dare to ask Mark if he were keeping anything from her about her life before Munich? It was enough to drive the sanest woman off her bloody rocker. Perhaps she'd never been on it in the first place. Issi closed her eyes and inhaled deeply.

The salt and heat filled her nostrils as they slid into her lungs. The rush and crash of the waves echoed in her ears. For a few spectacular seconds, there'd been no bomb, no brain injury, no Mark, and no stranger turning her world on its head.

Opening her eyes, Issi squinted as the sharp rays bounced off the sand and into her line of sight. Feeling more relaxed, she stepped onto the sand. The beach was free of bathers, but its waves lay dotted with surfers riding the swell.

Bliss.

A delicate calm filtered into her body.

Thoughts settled and her imagination quickened. The GOMA. She'd deal with all her issues later. Right now, she wanted to create until her fingers ached and her mind ran empty.

Filled with images and angles spread out in colors, Issi spun around with the intention of returning to her apartment and getting stuck into a new sculpture.

"Good morning."

A pair of hazel-green eyes and a smile with a dimple sitting plum in the center of his chin stopped Issi dead in her tracks.

"You!" She pointed a shaky finger at Cologne and Smiles man.

"I'm pleased to see you've recovered after yesterday." He

smiled again and she found it hard not to zero in on the familiar light in his eyes.

She knew those eyes.

She'd painted them.

Her brain ached.

"Who are you? Why are you following me?"

"Who are *you*, Issi?"

"I . . . I know who I am! The question here is who the bloody hell are you?" She stomped her foot on the sand and thrusted fisted hands onto her hips.

"I see your temper hasn't cooled off much." He stepped toward her.

Issi stepped back. "Don't you come any closer, asshole. Why. Are. You. Following. Me?" A flash of shock and pain crossed his eyes at her cussing him.

She hadn't meant to swear, but she was done with all the smoke and daggers. Now she wanted answers!

"You're asking all the wrong questions, Issi." He reached out a hand to touch her cheek and she pulled farther away from him. The invisible vise grip returned and squeezed her diaphragm, causing her to gasp for breath.

Movement at the top of the stairs leading to the beach caught her attention—*Mark*.

"Hey, you, step away from her. Do you hear me?" Mark ran down the steps and onto the sand. The humor of a man dressed in an expensive suit and wearing flashy Italian shoes while running on a beach did not escape her. Mark's skin was pale. The sun reflected off the thin sheen of perspiration lining his face. His eyes darted wildly between her and the stranger.

Who could she trust?

She didn't know this man whose eyes had haunted her for weeks. But Mark had recently shown her a side that she couldn't trust. Issi positioned herself at a distance between the two men.

The stranger's stance shifted from relaxed to battle-ready and caused a wave of urgency to surge through her veins. The ropes of muscle in his arms bulged and tensed, and his shoulders drew up as his legs shifted, like a tiger ready to pounce.

Issi noticed a tattoo of a soldier on one arm, and on the other . . .

"Ha!" Her hands clasped her mouth.

An arrow with red tail feathers just like the one on Mark's arm.

He caught her gaze, looked to where her eyes had fallen, then back to her. "Dutch Tulip Red. Your favorite color . . . or at least, it was." He ran a finger along the length of the tattoo. "And the name of the digger unit you betrayed—The Red Arrows." He turned a hateful gaze onto Mark.

"Mark, who is this?"

"I have no idea, but I'm sure he's trouble."

"Oh, it's 'Mark' now, is it?" The stranger squared his shoulder and moved forward with a menacing step. Mark and Issi instinctively shuffled back.

"I don't know you. You'd better leave or I'll call the cops." Mark's voice lacked his usual assuredness and urged Issi to assess the situation through new eyes.

The stranger knew them both—but how?

"Yes, please, call them. You know exactly who I am." The stranger's fists blanched as he balled them. Trouble was brewing.

"Babe, come here!" Mark commanded.

But instead of adhering to his call, she stood frozen to the spot, anxiety turning her blood to ice and her muscles to stone.

"No one forgets a traitor's face, Doyle!" Cologne and Smiles hit his left fist into his right hand, the sound causing Issi's body to jerk.

"I'm nothing of the sort. Isabella! Come here now!" Mark shouted at her, his eyes wild, his lips pale and his outstretched hand shaking.

"Isabella?" The stranger edged forward and to the left, making sure he stood halfway between Mark and herself. His hazel eyes took on a deep green, like moss after the rain, "You're no Isabella!"

Was he blocking her from Mark or from running away?

"Think a new name and different hair would wash away your sins?" he spat at Mark.

Mark shifted in the sand. His skin had paled even more and his lips turned a nasty tinge of grey.

"You've done a bloody good job of staying off the radar, but you fucked up when you took my—!"

The stranger's words whipped across the beach. Issi felt her legs turn to jelly as her mind swam and struggled through the quagmire engulfing her. She wasn't sure she'd heard that last word—why had her mind balked as he'd said it?

Mark's voice echoed across the sun baked beach, but nothing made sense anymore. Everything began to spin.

The stranger slowly stepped toward her and the world stood still. "Issi, look at me, please?" His words drifted toward her as though he were speaking through a muffled megaphone. With a touch as gentle as a morning breeze, he cupped her left cheek. His hand was callused but warm. Large and gentle.

"*I don't know if life is greater than death but love, my beloved Issi, is more than either.*"

The syllables and consonants struck true and echoed

across her mind. The poem she'd found on the internet the other day—the one she'd instantly loved.

Issi grabbed at her skull.

"God dammit, Isabella. Come on!" Mark made a move toward her.

"I wouldn't if I were you, mate. And stop calling her Isabella!" The stranger's warning rumbled like thunder.

Issi turned her head up. Her eyes refused to focus and her stomach pushed into her diaphragm.

As life returned to her numb limbs, the word the stranger had called her a few moments earlier struck home —wife!

No!

They were lying; this wasn't happening. Issi turned and sprinted up the steps.

"Isabella, wait!" Mark shouted as he darted in her direction, but Issi was already out of his grasp as she ran down the boardwalk, across the esplanade, and into the café.

Patrons shifted in their chairs and twisted to take in the frantic woman who'd stormed in and disrupted their meal.

"What the … you okay?" Jeff ran toward her.

Issi huffed and gasped. Her mouth opened, shut, and opened again as perspiration ran down her face and arms. Her head ached and her heart thumped her insides like the pounding waves on the shore.

"He … they …" She pointed to the road.

"Sam, get one of the girls to takeover. I'm driving Isabella home." Jeff instructed.

"No!" she gasped, and fell into his arms, unsettling some patrons at a table close by.

Sam trotted out of the kitchen, concern spread across his face. "What happened?"

"Not here," Jeff said softly.

"Get her home." Sam rubbed her back and handed Jeff the keys.

"Okay, we'll go to my place?" Jeff wrapped an arm around her, assuaging a fragment of her angst.

Issi nodded and Jeff guided her out through the kitchen.

"I'll finish up as soon I can." Sam wrapped his arms around them both and squeezed.

———

THE GUYS' house was situated a few kilometers away from the esplanade, near Mt Coolum. It sat on the top of the slope looking over the bustling seaside town and the ocean in the distance.

Jeff pulled into the garage and switched off the engine. "Come. I have just the thing." He smiled as he patted a hand on her knee.

Issi followed him inside. The décor resembled that of their café—sixties retro. But instead of the bright groovy colors of their eatery, they'd chosen an earthier palette for their home.

Issi stood in the lounge and gazed out through the balcony doors. The view of Coolum from above was breath-taking. Eucalyptus and Bunya trees towered over rooftops, highlighted every so often by bright orange blossoming poinciana trees. In the distance, a long container ship rode the deep blue ocean where it touched the edge of the world.

Standing in the corner beside the kitchen counter, Jeff opened a small bar fridge and pulled out a bottle, then reached for two shot glasses from the shelf above. "Drink this." He handed her one. "Tequila calms the nerves like nothing else."

Issi threw back her head and coughed as the famous Mexican drink burned its way down her throat.

"What happened? Did that no-good Mark try his luck with you?" His voice took on a stern tone as he waved them toward the lounge.

Issi sat on the plush brown leather couch and sighed. Where to begin.

"No . . . yes . . . ugh . . ." her curls fell against her cheeks when she shook her head.

She handed Jeff the shot glass, saying, "More please," then pressed her fingertips to her temples and rubbed.

Accepting her refill, she downed the second shot, then looked at her friend. His big brown eyes sat like large marbles in his face.

"I went down to the beach to get some fresh air . . ."

Jeff nodded and poured them both another shot, but left the filled glasses on the table.

"He appeared out of nowhere."

"Colognes and smiles? This is getting out of hand." Jeff stood, paced the length of the lounge and returned to his seat, "Is that why you ran?"

"Not right away. I argued with him." Issi thumped a fist on the coffee table.

"Was that wise? You didn't provoke him... Issi we have no idea who this man is..." Jeff stopped his rant when Issi held up her hand.

"No, he was strangely calm, warm even. He flipped it on me and told me I was asking all the wrong questions!"

Jeff pushed the shot toward her.

She downed it. The sharp liquid washed over her frazzled nerves, calming them and leaving her somewhat woozy. She caught her breath and told Jeff everything.

"Far out! You mean to say Smiles and Cologne knows

you, and Mark? What did Mark do?" Jeff placed her glass beside his but did not refill it.

"Mark ordered the man to stay away. He wanted me to go with him, but I couldn't. Something about the way that man looked at Mark told me I couldn't trust Mark."

"I knew it!" Jeff slapped a hand on his knee.

"He also eluded to Mark deserting from the army."

"Deserting? I didn't know Mark was in the army?" Jeff rubbed his chin with his left hand.

Issi leaned forward and grabbed Jeff's undrunk shot. "Neither did I. Bottoms up."

Her mate cocked an eyebrow at Issi then stood and placed the bottle on the counter. "What do you want to do?"

"Hide out here for now?"

"Absolutely! But we need to figure out who these ratbags are." He nodded and sat once more.

"There's something else . . ." Issi headed to the counter where she grabbed the bottle then poured them both another shot. "You'll need another too."

Jeff looked at the shot glass, then back at her, his gaze wary. "What else could there possibly be?"

Issi took a deep breath. "He called me his wife."

———

ISSI RUBBED her eyes and yawned.

"Have a good nap?" Jeff smiled from his seat on the couch across from her.

"Yeah, thanks. Those Tequilas knocked me." She proffered a cheeky grin. 'Mmm, what smells so good?" she sat up and glanced toward the kitchen.

"Green curried chicken." Jeff put down the television

remote, stood and walked to the kitchen when Issi's phone rang.

"Hey. How you goin?" Sam's voice sounded a little tense.

"Fine thanks. Something wrong? You sound a little stressed." Issi turned to face Jeff who gave her a concerned look.

"Erm... I have Cologne and Smiles here. Issi, he's desperate. Wants to know if you're okay...and..."

Her mates words caused her stomach to clench and the last of her nerves to go up in smoke."

"Can he come over and have a chat?" Sam sounded like a five year old asking for a scoop of ice crème before dinner.

"No." Issi simply wanted nothing to do with the stranger or Mark...Doyle whatever the lying ass's name was. Not today, not tomorrow, not bloody ever!

9

"Hey, lovely." Jeff strolled over to where Issi sat on their couch nursing a cup of coffee. "Sam and I are a little uncomfortable blowing this fella off every morning. It's been two days now." He twisted his hands and pranced from one foot to the other. "I think we should give him a chance." He raised his hands palms up when she made to say something. "Hear me out please. What harm could it do to listen to what he has to say? Especially if both Sam and I are with you?" Concern etched the corners of his eyes. "We don't mind having you here, it's just . . . this isn't you, lovely." He shrugged as his soft gaze travelled from her to his front door and back. "He might have all the answers you've been searching for."

Issi looked up to her friend now smiling back at her. "I know. But I'm scared, Jeff. What if he tells me about a life I wasn't happy in? How do I know he's telling me the truth and, maybe I wasn't a nice person. Or . . ."

She placed her coffee mug on the table before her, then clenched and unfolded her hands as she tried to convey all the questions which had been tumbling around the inside of her head for the last forty-eight hours.

"Now that I have the power to know, I'm not sure I want to. And . . . if he really is my husband . . ." She swallowed hard and shifted on the couch where she sat. ". . . do I have to go back to him—to being the wife of a man I don't even know? I've just ended one relationship- even if Mark was lying about it, and what about my life here, my art, you guys?"

"You don't have to do anything you don't want to. Sam and I will support you no matter what you decide." Jeff cocked his head as a warm smile spread across his face.

"We asked him to give you some space, but heck, Issi, if he is your husband, then there's a lot more to this story. It's important you sort it out."

"And what if he's a crackpot?" She shot back, not meaning to be bitchy, but . . . *Hell's bells! Can't everyone just leave me alone?*

"Sam and I will be here to throw him out on his ear and then we'll drive you straight to the police station to report him if he is one." He assured her.

She gritted her teeth. "So where's he been these last two years? Huh?"

"Ask him yourself." Jeff nodded toward the front door where Sam now stood with his hand balanced on the handle. "We love you, you know that, but it's time for some tough love. You can't hide away forever. All the answers to your questions are standing right there." Jeff waved toward his partner.

A click was followed by a draft, alerting Issi to the front door being opened. Smiles and Cologne guy stepped inside with a black satchel hanging from his right shoulder and a bunch of forget-me-nots in his hand. Sam proffered a sheepish grin then showed the man toward the lounge.

Issi's emotions walked a tight rope between anger toward her mates, excitement at seeing the stranger, and absolute fear. She sucked in a staggered breath and clenched her fists.

Sam walked over to her and sat before wrapping his arms around her. "We're desperate. We want our old friend back. We want the smiling happy, artistic *you* back."

"And you think allowing him inside your home will do that?" She slipped from his embrace, stood and folded her arms across her chest and pinched her fists beneath her elbows.

The man squeezed the fresh bunch of blooms into the glass holding the previous days' deposits. He looked up and smiled. Issi's knees threatened mutiny as he stood quietly beside the kitchen bench. His lips pulled tight and his hazel-green eyes, rimmed by shadows, held a cornucopia of uncertainties.

"Take a breath." Jeff came to stand beside her. "You're safe, I promise. Sam and I won't leave you alone. And by the looks of it, he's hurting. Hear him out."

"I'll make some coffee." Sam made his way into the kitchen.

"Tell me everything." Issi had summoned her sternest frown and hoped her voice backed her demand, wishing it was late enough in the day for tequila. Perhaps she'd be able to conjure a memory if she looked at him hard enough, to force her grey matter to quicken, to think back, to see their life together. Them and their family, her . . . A soft thrumming began in the back of her skull, warning her she was pushing too hard. Turning, she sat.

"Sit down, Tristan." Jeff waved toward the opposite couch.

Tristan, is it?

He took a seat and leaned forward with his elbows resting on his knees. Issi gave Jeff another stern look.

"I wasn't going to let some nameless guy waltz into my house. And before you get your knickers in a knot, Sam and I had a quick chat with him yesterday on our way out. Okay?" Jeff shrugged.

Issi answered with a slow nod, then turned her focus back to Tristan.

His lips were pale and he kept rubbing his hands together as his shoulders crept closer to his ears. Like her, he was afraid, unsure, and had suffered.

Sam returned with a tray of mugs, a jug of milk, and sugar. He placed it on the table in the center of the lounge and retook his spot on the arm of the couch beside Issi.

"I'm not sure exactly where to start . . ." Tristan stumbled over his words.

"From the beginning," Issi blurted, then pursed her lips and shook her head. "I have no past. I don't know who my parents were . . . are, or anything about . . . us. And why do you call me Issi?" She slowed when the volume of her voice increased along with her heart rate.

"Okay." He nodded, reached for a mug and poured some milk, then grabbed a teaspoon and stirred slowly as though he needed time to process her questions.

"Yes, you have a family. I've always called you Issi. Since the day you and your family moved here—er, I mean, to Victoria, from South Africa. Issi is short for Isolde."

Issi's world spun and the throbbing in her head increased its pace. Nausea roiled in her belly. How could this be?

"Isolde?" She managed before she buried her head between her knees.

"She's okay, mate." Jeff said as a strong warm hand rubbed her back.

I . . . sol . . . de . . . She rolled the name, *her name*, over in her mind then whispered it to herself as if it would make a difference. *"Isolde."* It tasted foreign, felt out of place, but weirdly, it sounded right. She caught her breath and straightened. The expression on Tristan's face shook her to her core.

"I couldn't begin to explain how hard it is to grasp the fact that you are close to people I don't even know. That two strangers are comforting you instead of me. We used to be everything to one another. I know you inside and out, and you know—*knew* me better than I ever did."

Tears burned the back of Issi's eyes. His heartfelt words chipped away at her shattered heart. "You're right. I could never understand." But for some reason she could feel it in the depths of her very being—a connection, a knowing beyond knowing, and a loss.

Tristan wiped the back of his hand across his eyes and took a long sip from his mug. "I have proof." He reached into his satchel and pulled out a folder. From it, he unpacked a stack of letter-head sized pages.

"Here is your birth certificate and our marriage certificate." He handed Issi the papers. Her eyes trotted over the names printed in black as her fingers clasped the crisp white leaves of the copied documents.

"Here is your favorite wedding photo of us." He handed her a photograph where they stood nose to nose, her face cupped in his hands and a vineyard spreading out around them.

The air stilled and her lungs froze. Bile burned her

throat and threatened to roll into her mouth in a wave of bitter disbelief.

"I'm sorry . . . is this . . .?" Tristan began and Issi stopped him by raising a hand.

After a moment, when the ground stilled and the air softened enough for her to be able to suck in a few mouthfuls, Issi looked up.

"I'm not Isabella Irish from Applecross, Perth, WA." She repeated to herself as though it would remind her of who she really was. "You're showing me I'm Isolde Rivalen of Mildura, Victoria?"

Tristan nodded. "Yeah, formerly Van Rooyen, from Constantia in South Africa."

The name tickled her frantic thoughts, and she ignored her mates gasps as her mind raced onto the next puzzle piece.

This explains my accent.

She motioned for Tristan to continue.

"You were born there, in the Cape's wine lands, but when you were eight, your parents decided to move to Australia with you and your then three-year-old sister."

Issi swallowed hard. "I—I have a sister?"

Tristan nodded. "Yeah. Miranda. You are . . . very close."

"Do they know?" Issi felt an invisible hand clutch at her heart.

"That you're alive?" Tristan shifted in his seat and placed his undrunk coffee on the table. "It's complicated."

Issi swallowed as both Jeff and Sam lay strong muscled arms around her. Tristan's gaze followed their movements. His lips pursed then relaxed.

"Then uncomplicate it."

"Only Miranda and her husband do. We have not yet told your mother."

"My mother . . . and my father?" Issi did not like the look that flashed across Tristan's face at her question. Somewhere in the dark recesses of her heart, broken memories were putting two and two together.

Tristan inhaled and rubbed a hand over his short cropped hair. "Your father was killed in a home invasion two years ago." He paused and waited.

"A home invasion, in Mildura?" Issi tried to make sense of what he was saying.

"No. South Africa. He'd returned to your family farm in Constantia. The men broke in, stole nothing, but shot him and left. The police labelled it a home invasion."

"Lovely, what was the name of that artist's painting you bought?" Jeff whispered cautiously.

"Va-Van Rooyen." Her lips mouthed the words but her voice hid in the back of her throat.

"You have one of your dad's paintings?" Tristan asked, half-excited.

Issi nodded as she digested the information. "What else?"

"Your parents separated a few years after their immigration. Your dad couldn't assimilate and your mother refused to return to a country drowning in corruption and violence." Tristan paused considered her, then continued, "Your parents didn't sell their wine farm in Constantia but had also made a success of the vineyard in Mildura. So Glynis stayed and Herman left. They never divorced, but they never got back together either. He visited regularly." Tristan paused as he grappled for words.

He shifted in his seat and his gaze focused on the wall behind her as though her life were playing like a cinema reel in the background.

Issi leaned into the couch as her world crumbled to the floor.

"If my mom has lost so much, why keep me from her?" Issi almost pleaded.

"I had to make sure." Tristan reached forward and gripped the rim of his coffee mug, the tips of his fingers turning it this way and that.

A cool breeze rose off the ocean and brought with it the soft scent of eucalyptus as it wafted through the open balcony doors.

Issi raised her chin and closed her eyes for a moment, then sighed, "Sure of what?" She sat on her hands when they began to shake.

"That it was you, and of how deeply you were involved . . ."

"Involved?" Her stomach clenched and the bile threatened to burn a hole in her throat.

"With Doyle and his dealings." Tristan glanced at her then returned to staring at his coffee mug.

"Dealings? Who is Mark . . . Doyle . . . whoever? And how do you know him?" Sam piped up, clearly no longer able to remain silent.

Tristan straightened slowly, never taking his eyes off of her as though he might lose her if he did. "He was a corporal in my brigade."

"Brigade?" Jeff gripped his hands together as he shifted forward on his seat.

Tristan considered them, his eyes returning to Issi as he searched her face. "It's hard you know . . . to look at the woman who knew and loved my deepest secrets, every inch of me, better than I knew myself and realize . . ."

"What?" Frustration poked fun at her patience.

"You think I'm a stranger. It's impossible to comprehend

that our entire life before that bomb has simply been wiped from your existence."

A pain-filled silence wrapped itself around them. Issi fought the strange urge to jump over the coffee table standing between them and into his arms—it felt like the natural thing to do, as though she'd done it a thousand times before. At the same time, she wanted to run down the street screaming like a mad woman, pulling at her hair. This was too much. The pain in his eyes . . . Why couldn't she remember?

"We were posted in Iran for a time. Doyle was never much of a team player. He'd already received a warning and the guys didn't trust him. When you're there, in enemy territory, you must trust each person has the others' backs, and we did, except . . ."

"He didn't," she finished.

A smile crept across Tristan's face. God, it was a beautiful sight. Issi wished for her clay as her fingers itched to trace the soft skin of his lips and neck . . . torso . . . and . . . She focused on his eyes. The hazel had softened and the green brightened with . . . hope?

"I love that you still do that."

"What?" She blushed.

"Finish my sentences." Something twinkled in his eyes as he lowered his gaze.

The effect rippled through Issi, who shifted uncomfortably. It was hard to dismiss the brewing chemistry between them.

Sam who broke the moment. "Do you want Jeff and me to stay or are you happy if we make a quick trip to the café? We'll be on our phones."

Issi sighed and wiped a hand over her face. She didn't

know this man with his stories and papers proving a truth she had no memory of.

Something about Tristan stirred a trust, an ingrained knowledge she would be safe with him. She couldn't explain it, but neither could she ignore it. Considering her mates then Tristan.

"I'm good. Go, thanks." She squeezed Sam's hand then twisted to hug Jeff.

As the guys closed the front door, Issi swallowed before turning her attention back to Tristan. "The army?" She lifted her chin and sat back in the couch, cold mug of coffee cupped in her hands.

Tristan's shoulder relaxed and the pallor of his skin drew some color. "We were assigned as a protection detail to move antiquities from a small town to Bandar Abbas on the south-eastern coast of Iran. Our convoy was ambushed while transporting the priceless objects to safety. It was only afterward we realized he was missing."

"Mark?" Issi sat up straight.

"Doyle, and yeah. Once we were extracted and returned to base, questions were asked. Doyle was AWOL and two of my men were dead. My CO and I started digging and discovered evidence he had ties to a huge antiquities and human trafficking ring, but by then he'd vanished without a trace. Doyle got away with millions of dollars' worth of Eastern heritage."

"And me? Why me? How did he find me when you couldn't?" Issi was no longer able to sit. She shimmied forward, plonked her mug on the table, and began pacing the short space between the balcony doors and the couch.

"I thought you were dead. The bloody German authorities gave us a body to bury, for the love of God." Tristan clenched his fists and shifted in his seat.

"But how did Doyle convince them I was his fiancée?" she blurted, then froze when Tristan's face fell and his lips turned a deathly white.

"Fiancée?"

Issi nodded and came to sit again as her knees turned to mush.

"Did you . . . Did he . . . fiancée . . ." Tristan swallowed and his hands wove together as he attempted to articulate what was clearly not easy for him to ask.

"Not that it has anything to do with you, but no," Issi answered the unspoken question. "It never felt right . . . him and I. He tried, believe me, but no."

Tristan's head rolled back as he pushed both his hands through his short ash-blond hair. "Thank God."

"But that doesn't answer what I asked you. How did he get his claws into me?" Issi pushed on even as the thumping in her head increased in intensity.

Tristan's lips pulled tight as though he'd smelled something rotten. "He knew of you. How he found you . . . I don't know, but this is where things get tricky."

"How so?" Issi asked, not liking the seriousness of his tone.

"To put it simply, Interpol's been watching you," Tristan confessed.

"What!" she all but shouted.

"It has to do with Doyle. One of their investigators managed to track him down shortly before I found you."

Issi's world began to spin once again.

"Look, I know this is a lot to take in and we haven't even scraped the tip of the iceberg Can we go for a walk to the water? You used to love long walks to help clear your mind. And from what I've seen, you still do.

His confession rocked her world a little more and Issi

felt herself tipping over the edge of a dark, scary precipice. "How long have you and the bloody international police been watching me?" She stood and moved away from where he remained seated.

"Interpol—a while. Me, around two weeks."

The words punched Issi in the gut as she staggered backwards. "I think you should leave."

"But . . ." Tristan jumped to his feet and stepped toward her.

"Go, Tristan. This is too much! I don't know you. I don't know me!" Issi wrapped her arms around herself.

"But you have to give me a chance to finish. I know you, and I know deep down you remember me!" Tristan pleaded. "I understand how frightening this must be for you. Please, Issi, please . . . I failed you, but on my life, I'll never let anyone hurt you ever again."

His words very nearly brought her to her knees as she pointed to the door.

Every part of her begged to be thrown into this stranger's arms. Her heart began to remember him, even longed for him, and her body reacted in ways she'd not known possible when he looked at her and smiled. But her mind would not allow it.

Mark . . . Doyle, had lied to her all this time. So how could she trust this man who'd been hiding in the shadows with her truth tucked in his back pocket?

Tristan's shoulders dropped as he turned and stumbled toward the door. "I won't give up on you, Issi. *I don't know if life is greater than death. But love is more than either.*"

The words echoed through her heart and washed over the scar tissue in her brain.

Remember!

10

Issi squinted into the burgeoning dawn as she stepped out onto the balcony of her mates' apartment. She'd not slept a wink. The information dump that had landed in her lap yesterday left her tired and testy.

Movement to the far left, along the road, drew her attention. A man wearing a hoodie over a cap and a pair of shades spun clumsily away when he saw her. He moved backward, stumbled, then trotted off. Something about the way he held himself sent a chill down her spine. If that was an Interpol agent, he sucked. Issi opened her mouth to shout something to him when her blood froze . . . Was that Mark?

I'll always know where you are... Mark's voice chilled her insides.

"Coffee?" Jeff called from inside.

Issi almost jumped the railing.

"Sorry, lovely. Didn't mean to startle you."

"It's all good." She added half a smile so her friend didn't think she was weird. "Yes please."

She returned her attention to the gorgeous morning and

slowed her breathing. In the distance, a pandemonium of cockatoos squawked and cackled as they fed on the local Bunya trees. Sun sprites danced across the ocean on the far horizon and the humidity wafted off the waves and blanketed the seaside suburb in a sticky haze. Gosh, she loved this place.

But her bliss ebbed. There, standing across the road, waiting, stood Tristan—the man who claimed to be her husband. Gripped in his left hand, the flowers.

Her stupid brain had run their conversation on repeat the entire night and then melted into a migraine from hell.

After he'd left, she'd wanted to kick herself for being so emotional. She'd not given herself time to ask about them, about her past, her family.

"Breathe," she whispered.

Mark had not returned any of the texts she'd sent after she'd kicked Tristan out yesterday afternoon. He'd been a part of her life for two years, and while he'd started acting like an asshat in the last few weeks, he'd always prioritized her best interests— or so she'd believed. The problem was she had no way to verify what Tristan had told her. Her head, which called for logic and proof, warred with her heart, that wanted it to be true.

"The head a little better?" Jeff plodded out onto the balcony holding two mugs.

"It's a little foggy." She rubbed the scarred patch behind her left ear then took the steaming mug offered by her friend. "Thanks."

"Why don't you invite him up for coffee?" Jeff gestured with his chin toward Tristan who stood like a lovelorn puppy on the sidewalk below.

Issi considered her mate's words, but her fear kicked against it.

"Invite him yourself." She stubbornly turned her back on the rising sun and her forlorn husband.

Her hard-ass attitude would not be tolerated by either of the guys, but she couldn't help herself. She was afraid and exhausted and angry, and a myriad of other emotions ... but most of all she was lost. So very lost. And heck, not everyone had their memory ripped from their brain only to find out the things she had the last few days. Surely she was allowed to throw one small tantrum?

Jeff winked and smiled then leaned against the balustrade. "Come up for a cuppa, mate."

"Cheeky bugger!" she mock-scolded.

Jeff let out a hearty laugh. "It's for your own good. By the sounds of it, you both still have a lot to work out—so pull up your big girl undies and get to it." He kissed her on her forehead before he downed his coffee.

"Thanks." She squeezed her mate's arm. "You and Sam are my rocks."

"Always," he whispered and made his way back to the bedroom.

Issi stood by the open front door waiting for Smiles and cologne man.

"Hi." Tristan beamed as he stretched out a shaky fistful of flowers toward her.

If she was being honest with herself, she was excited to see him again, but she also dreaded receiving any more shocking news.

"Hi. Thanks." She took the flowers, and waved him inside, trying her best to hide the tremble in her own hands. "Take a seat." Issi nodded toward the high chair at the kitchen counter. "I'll put on a fresh pot of coffee."

"You two gonna be okay? There's food in the fridge, or

feel free to come to the café for a feed when you need a breather." Sam strode out of the bedroom.

"Yeah, today's muscle pot hump day," Jeff added, coming to stand with his arm around his partner.

"We'll see. Thanks, guys." Issi gave them both a hug.

"Okay, well, you know where to find us." A frown crossed Jeff's brow as he gave her knowing glance.

Issi poured herself and Tristan a coffee. "Hungry?"

"No thanks. I grabbed something before I came over." He gifted her his gorgeous smile and suddenly the world around her brightened a little.

Tristan sat at the kitchen bench, mug of coffee in hand, and Issi leaned her bum against the stove. She placed the fresh bunch of flowers in a cup of water on the counter behind her with the two other glasses filled with flowers.

"Why them?" She nodded toward the pretty blooms.

"They were . . . are your favorites. You hand-painted this for me and I wore it every time I left for training or on deployment." Tristan tugged on a silver chain around his neck; dangling from it was an oval charm. "I haven't taken it off since . . . I buried you, or thought I buried you."

Molded into the silver base of the charm was a porcelain background. Painted on the porcelain, a single forget-me-not.

Tears burned the back of her eyes—she couldn't remember, so why did it mean so much to her?

"Have you taken time off from the army to be here?" She twisted her fingers as she forced her voice not to warble over the words.

"No. I'm in the reserves now and spend most of my time in the vineyards." He twirled the cup with one hand just as he had the day before.

"You're a wine farmer?"

Tristan sighed deeply. "Yes." His lips tightened across his face and the hazel in his eyes deepened.

"I'm sorry." She placed her mug on the counter then wiped sweaty hands on her pant legs.

"For what?" His voice deepened.

"I know it must be extremely tedious to tell me things you think that I should know."

She considered this ex-digger-come-wine-farmer. Her husband.

Tristan didn't answer. Issi guessed he was unsure how to verbalize his feelings without hurting her.

She used the moment to take in his full form. He was dressed like a local in surf shorts and a branded surfing top, his shades balanced on his head.

He was easy on the eye.

Crew-cut, dusty blond hair. Strong jaw and dimples in all the right places, not to mention eyes as dreamy as if they were straight out of a romance novel. He was a head taller than her with a solid body and broad shoulders. He had a quiet demeanor, one which reminded her of a calm ocean— flat and deep with many treasures hidden beneath the surface.

"I'm sorry about yesterday. It was all a little much." She apologized over the rim of her mug.

"It was my fault. I moved too fast, gave you too much information at once." Tristan continued to twist and turn the mug.

"Tell me more. How did we meet? When did we get married?" Issi decided to tackle the questions which had bothered her most.

"Your family moved to Mildura when you were a young girl. My family's vineyard bordered yours. We were instant mates, and by the time we entered our last year of high school, I knew there was no one else in this world I was meant to share my life with."

Issi swallowed hard as his words filled the gaps in her mind and soothed her confused heart. "How long have we been married?" she asked as she rinsed out her empty cup before coming to the opposite side of the counter and folding her arms.

Tristan looked at her. His gaze swam with hope and uncertainty. "Six years . . . and then . . ." He wiped a hand over his face. "Married eight years in total. I waited for you to finish your degree in art. In fact, that was your father's prerequisite while I was actively serving."

My father. Her mind repeated, as her heart jolted.

"It was the day after your graduation. You refused to wait a moment longer. You were twenty-four."

"And you?"

"We're the same age." The hint of a smile pierced his serious expression.

Issi chewed on her bottom lip as another question surfaced. "Do we ha-have children?"

Tristan shook his head and Issi held her breath when his face paled and his lips thinned. "We were struggling. It was probably the only time we ever fought."

"Fought?" she whispered.

"You blamed yourself." Tristan paused and cautiously reached out to lay his hand on hers. "We suffered two miscarriages. One a few months before the bombing." The callouses etched into his fingers and palm chafed her skin as his grip tightened.

Issi paused as she digested the revelations. Just when she'd hoped there would be no more surprises . . .

"I'm sorry. Do you want me to leave?" he asked, pulling away.

She stopped herself from reaching out to grab back the hand he'd retracted. Some part of her needed him to comfort her, to have him hold her, to tell her it was all going to work out.

Instead, she allowed her left hand to briefly touch her belly as she steeled her emotions. "Don't be. I can't remember." She shook her head, pushing away the odd sensation finding its way to the surface. "As a reservist, do you still get called to active duty?" Better to steer them away from the subject.

A look of concerned relief washed over Tristan's face. "Only if needed, but I get called up for training a few times a year. The 4th Brigade has to remain battle-ready at all times."

"When you're not training?"

"I spend time in the vineyard and used to watch . . ." His voice cracked.

It was her turn to console him. "It's okay. This can't be easy for you either."

Tristan turned his coffee mug once again, swallowed hard, then finished his sentence. "To watch you paint and create those sculptures while I did the books for the business. The way your hands caressed the clay and the look in your bright blue eyes carried me far away from the here and now as you showed me other worlds . . . Sorry, I sound weird." He wiped the back of his free hand across his eyes.

"You're not." Issi came to stand beside Tristan before cupping his face in her hands. "I dreamt of you . . . your eyes." The warmth of his skin caressed her palms and her thumbs ached to reach across and stroke the red plumpness of his lips.

Tristan hissed as he inhaled deeply. "It's been a lonely two years." He stroked the side of her face with the very tip of his index finger. Issi closed her eyes and willed her mind to forage deeper for the lost moments of the past, but all she found was a distant darkness pounding its way to the present.

Her head spun and throbbed. The air in the house felt suddenly oppressive, and she made her way out onto the balcony. Tristan followed.

He sighed and stood with his back against the railings, arms folded across his broad chest. "It feels like a dream."

Issi turned to look at him.

"To me . . . to anyone who ever knew you . . . you've been dead for two years. For two long, dark years I've walked to your grave every morning, placed a fresh bunch of your favorite flowers in the vase on your headstone, and returned to say goodnight at dusk." His Adam's apple bobbed up and down. "And now here I am, facing the impossible: standing beside my dead wife."

"I-I don't know what to say. It might feel unreal to you . . . but to me it's all a jumble of stories and mixed feelings . . . I need to know more, please?"

"Look I want nothing more than to tell you all about us, your family, and to move forward, but . . ."

"My family . . ."

Tristan twisted to face her and placed his hands on her shoulders. "Didn't your friends think it was weird that you sound nothing like someone whose grown up in Australia?"

Issi shook her head. "The specialists in Munich . . . at least, Mark told me that's what they said . . ." Issi's anger returned.

"Said what?"

"They blamed it on my injury. Tell me more about my family please?" she pleaded.

Tristan sighed deeply. "There is so much catching up to do, but it has to wait."

"Why?" Issi fought back her tears. She had a sister, parents . . .

"Issi, Doyle's dangerous—far more than you could ever imagine." He paused and she took her time to understand what it was he was trying to explain.

Mark? Dangerous?

He had freaked her out in those last days before the showdown on the beach. "You're saying dangerous as in, can-seriously-harm-a-person dangerous? "

Tristan nodded. "Yes. I don't want any family up here while he's on the loose."

"And what if . . . would he hurt my family?" And might her harm her? A million questions drizzled in fear zoomed around the inside of her mind and came to rest in her heart.

Tristan pursed his lips, dropping his head, then looked back at her. "I believe they're safe for now. I've asked the Interpol agent if he were able to arrange some security without them being noticed."

"Interpol?" Issi swallowed.

"They're gathering evidence on Mark. I'm not sure how close they are to making an arrest—when they locate him, that is. But I do know that they need him to lead them to a bigger fish. Would you consider a sit down with the lead investigator? He is after some answers and you require protection until Doyle is found and arrested."

Issi leaned forward with her hands on her knees. She drew in a deep breath and cautiously controlled her exhale.

"Are you okay?" Tristan's hand came to rest on her back, warm and comforting.

"Yeah. It's just so much . . . Is that part of why you and

Miranda decided to keep the news of me being alive from everyone until you knew all was safe?"

"Yes, and I needed time to figure out what was going on with you," he confessed.

Issi straightened her body. "Why not simply knock on my door and ask me? If you thought I was in danger, why wait? Surely I had a right to know sooner rather than later!" She slammed balled fists onto her hips.

A soft, knowing smile spread across Tristan's face. "I missed you so much!"

"Yeah? From where I'm standing, you sure took your time to show me." She was being unreasonable, but from her point of view, this was a lot to swallow.

"From where I was standing, you'd been dead for two years. Then I discovered you were alive and living in the company of a criminal."

"But he was there when I woke up. He cared for me, took me home . . . to Isabella's home, or what was left of it. He settled the estate. He's the reason I am who I am," Issi exclaimed.

"Yeah. That's another thing."

"What is?" Issi's anger twisted around her anxiety and burned.

"The police in WA suspect there was more to the fire than a simple electrical fault."

Issi slid onto the floor. "It was him—Ma—Doyle, wasn't it?" She rested her head on her hands and Tristan sat beside her.

"They think so."

"To hide the real Isabella's life from me?" Issi swallowed as the pieces began to fall in place.

"You are *you*, Issi, and that man . . ." Tristan wrapped an arm around her, ". . . has nothing to do with who you are.

You are still the woman with a heart of gold, and fingers that create magic. Even if you can't, I still see you in you. You're just lost, that's all. Take my hand, my love. I know the way."

A sharp stab of pain sliced through the center of her head and pooled at the base of her neck as the world began to spin.

Issi shrugged off his arm and tried to stand, but her legs gave way. Before she could fall, Tristan collected her in his arms and carried her to the bedroom.

———

"HERE WE GO." Tristan handed her a cool, wet washer with one hand while holding back her hair with the other.

A thumb stroked the base of her scar and she held her breath, waiting for him to say something. When he didn't, she closed her eyes as he leaned and placed a soft kiss against the melted, contorted skin that was her ear.

Not even the guys had been allowed a glimpse of her scars, yet this single gesture from a man who'd loved her all his life sent the Milky Way rippling through her body and across her soul.

He dropped her hair and straightened, as she opened her eyes and wiped the wet cloth across her mouth. "I thought the stupid migraine was gone . . . but . . ." She leaned over the toilette bowl and wretched again.

"Is there anything I can get you from the pharmacy?" Tristan asked, his voice laced with concern and helplessness.

Issi shook her head. "No thanks. I need rest... no bright lights . . . I think I'm okay now." She struggled to her feet.

Tristan wrapped an arm around her waist and helped

her to the basin before letting go. She wiped her face then rinsed her mouth.

"Come, you need to lie down."

"Don't we need to meet with that investigator?" Issi's world spun.

"It can wait." He guided her out of the bathroom and to the spare bedroom where he laid her down, then, as though it was the natural thing to do, he slid in behind her and pulled her into his warm, hard body.

Issi's throbbing head told her to push him away. Who did he think he was, taking advantage like this—but her heart shushed it. Her instincts confirmed that Tristan, unlike Doyle, would not harm her and another part recognized that she was finally where she belonged.

Tristan shifted then tugged on her shoulder to get her to turn and face him. Issi squinted as their faces came nose to nose. Tristan gently stroked an index finger up her cheek and down her jaw.

"You're sure he won't harm anyone else?" She couldn't let go of the fear that Mark would go to any lengths to get her back.

"Yes. It's you he wants. He's still hanging around here somewhere."

Tristan's words struck a chord.

"What? Has he tried to contact you?" He frowned and leaned away.

"This morning, before you arrived," she pushed up on her elbow, " I was out on the balcony. There was a man dressed in surf shorts and a hoodie. I couldn't see his face, but-" Issi fell back on her pillow when her head spun and her stomach lurched.

Tristan pulled her into him. "I'll get onto it. I swear no

one will ever harm you again. I've failed you once—I never will again."

Issi pushed away and angled her head. The look on his face was that of a weeping angel. Her heart broke. Dripping from his eyes were worlds of regret, anger, and self-loathing. She slowly leaned in and did the only thing that could make it a little easier. Resting one hand where his heart thrummed like a war drum, she lowered her face and kissed away the tears trickling down his cheeks. Their saltiness soaked her lips and sealed a promise she knew she'd made but could not remember—a commitment she had given and received once upon a time, long ago.

"No one could have protected me from that bomb. Don't blame yourself for the evil deeds of others." She laid one last kiss on his lips.

Tristan's arms snaked around her body and a hand cupped the back of her head as their kiss intensified—a kiss she'd waited her whole new life to share.

Tristan pulled away then tucked her neatly into the hollow of his body before whispering into her ear, "We'll sort it all out later. Sleep."

11

Issi followed Tristan across the street, like a mole creeping out of its hole.

"It feels good to get out again." She flipped the strap of her handbag over her shoulder with one hand while the other gripped a duffel bag. Dear, sweet Jeff had packed more than a week's worth of clothing for her the day after she'd come sprinting frantically into their café.

Now they were on their way to meet with the Interpol investigator and then, most likely, her place. Her world had turned inside out during the last week.

"How's the head?" Tristan asked as he opened the door of his rental car for her.

"Better, thanks." She slipped into the front passenger seat.

The day was steamy and overcast, but the sweat forming on her forehead and beneath her arms was more from nerves than the humidity.

Her migraine had subsided late the previous afternoon, and Tristan had stayed for dinner. The guys had enjoyed his company. Tristan had revealed more of himself, and she'd discovered she liked his funny quirks. He'd had them all in stitches during the course of their meal, regaling them with stories of back home. He was careful, she'd noticed, to avoid anything that would upset her. At one point during their chatter, Issi had realized she felt more at home in her skin than she ever had.

"Let's go," Tristan said as he closed his door and started the engine of the small hatchback.

"Where are we meeting him?" she asked, wiping her hands on her cotton baby blue shorts.

"His hotel in Noosa."

The drive was quiet except for a woman's gorgeous crooning which played via the car speakers from his phone.

"Who is this?"

"Sarah Calderwood—she's a local Queenslander and one of your favorites. She often performs at theaters all over Australia, and I flew you up one year for our anniversary to watch her in the Celtic Spirit performance at QPAC." He didn't glance at her, but kept his eyes glued to the road before him.

"Oh."

"You had all her music on your old iPod which you refused to chuck, even when I got you a new phone," he added as he turned the car onto the esplanade.

Issi leaned her head back and closed her eyes as the alternative folk music danced into her ears and seeped into her blood. The tips of her fingers began to tingle and the vision of a red-bricked building surrounded by blossoming bushes of forget-me-nots appeared in her mind's eye.

"You planted them around my studio," she said, not opening her eyes.

"What?" His voice was hoarse and when she rolled her head to the left and opened her eyes, she was met by a soul contorted in pain.

"The forget-me-nots . . ."

Tristan didn't reply but the sound of his sharp inhale told her she'd found a piece of her past with his help. Her heart soared.

———

SHUFFLING into the far corner of the elevator Issi instinctively reached for Tristan's hand. She felt safe with him by her side, but she missed Jeff and Sam and wished they had been able to come along. It was peak season at the café, and they simply weren't able to take time off.

It was peak season everywhere.

Noosa was a prime getaway spot and there were holiday-makers all over the place. Everything smelled of sunscreen, and excited children's squeals echoed off the walls in the foyer of the hotel. Thankfully the lift was empty, until it stopped two floors below their destination. A bulky family dressed in swimmers, wearing hats, and carrying boogie boards, towels, and a sun umbrella clambered in.

"Erm, we're going up." Tristan pointed to the roof with his index finger.

"S'okay. The bloody things are so busy, we'll tag along for the ride before we go our own way," the pudgy puce-colored man replied. Two boys giggled then began to play, punch-pushing into Issi.

The sunburnt father twisted on his heel and grumbled over his shoulder, "No more from you two."

Issi glanced at the boys. One of them gave her a cheeky

grin which caused his plump apple-like cheeks to squish and bulge. The sharp mixture of sweat and coconut plugged up her nose. Tristan's words about their battle with fertility surfaced and a subtle sadness echoed in the hollows of her heart.

The elevator stopped and the door slid open. Issi and Tristan pushed their way past the family and out onto the warmly lit passageway of the fifth floor. She inhaled the musty yet somewhat fresher air of the hotel, and Tristan waved for her to follow.

"This way. Room five-o-nine." He took her hand in his.

Issi glanced at their entwined fingers. A thrill ran through her body. She wanted to sculpt this image, immortalize it in clay. Her brain imprinted the lines and shadows as the pair walked on. Yes, this would be her next project after the GOMA.

"Here we are." Tristan stopped them in front of the hotel door then knocked. Issi's nerves began firing like an electric storm. They were here to discuss Doyle, but how much of his shady dealings had he made her complicit in?

The lock clicked and the door opened to reveal a bright friendly, olive-skinned face and a pair of twinkling dark eyes.

"Come in. I'm Thomas Campbell. Pleased to meet you, Mrs. Rivalen. Good to see you again, Tristan." A man who stood as tall as Tristan, but whose accent sounded extremely similar to hers, held out his hand. Issi paused. She wasn't used to being called Mrs., let alone Rivalen.

"Oh, I'm sorry. Forgive me." His eyes darted between her and Tristan.

"No worries. Call me . . . Issi." She smiled and took his hand.

They made their way into the suite and Thomas closed the door.

"This is my wife, Rochelle Campbell. I hope you don't mind, Issi, but I asked Rochelle, who is a medical doctor, to sit with us today. While she's not a neurologist, she does have experience in the field of PTSD. She's one of the best trauma doctors you'll ever meet. There is a lot we must discuss." Thomas eluded to her injury, but Issi's mind still battled to get over the words *Mrs. Rivalen.*

"Thomas, you don't need to sell me." The woman flapped a hand at her husband. "He simply wanted to make sure we had enough support in place for you."

His wife was stunning. Her milky-white hair had a rainbow colors streaked through it, and her eyes were the shade of a tropical ocean. Like Tristan, her demeanor was calming and Issi felt safe in her presence at once.

"Do you assist your husband in all his investigations?" Tristan asked as he eyed her.

"Ah. No. I simply tagged along because I've never been to Australia before and, well . . . when he discovered the extent of Issi's injuries, he asked if I'd mind helping. If you're not comfortable with that I can leave, but please know I take confidentiality seriously." She assured Tristan who nodded.

"Thanks."

"I appreciate you taking the time to help us." Issi smiled.

"Sorry. I know it's not comfortable." Thomas waved them toward the small round table with four seats that stood in the far corner of the one-bedroom hotel suite. "But I think it is better we are not seen together. Not until I have a handle on what is going on."

The statement sent a trickle of fear tumbling along Issi's spine.

She scanned her surroundings as she digested all the new information. "Your accents, they sound familiar."

"Thomas and I are both South African. In fact, I grew up on a wine farm not too far from your father's—our condolences. It can't have been easy then or now."

Rochelle's sincerity was touching. The blonde doctor took her seat and Issi wondered if they had met under different circumstances, they might have become friends.

"I don't remember him," Issi said simply, then sat.

She focused on the jug sitting center to the table, a small cheese platter beside it. Her gaze followed the tiny droplets of water as they trickled down the belly of the of the glass vessel containing juice, in an attempt to prevent her world from spinning off its axis again.

"It bothers you that you can't remember?" Rochelle leaned forward and placed a warm hand on hers. "That's okay, but don't feel guilty about it."

"It's like I know that I should know things, but I don't. If I had to compare it to anything, it would be like staring into a dark bottomless hole on a starless night," Issi explained.

"When all this is sorted out, I know of an excellent neurologist in Sydney who's using groundbreaking technology and medicine for people with many different kinds of brain injuries. He's a colleague from my days with Doctors Without Borders. I can certainly put you in touch with him if you'd like?" Rochelle offered.

Issi swallowed. She'd thought there was nothing more anyone could do for her—that was what the doctors and Mark had told her. "Thank you. I would appreciate that."

"Right. We need to get down to business." Thomas urged.

"So you want more information about Mark?"

"Yes. I've been tracking the man you know as Mark

Cornwall—Doyle Morhold—for around eighteen months now. He is one step beneath the evil men who sit behind a trafficking ring the likes of which the world has never known," Thomas shuffled some papers beside his laptop.

"Trafficking ring?" Issi asked, flabbergasted.

"Yes. But not unlike an octopus, the true head of the beast has many arms—illegal art trafficking is just one," He shrugged as his right index finger pointed his notes.

Issi's stomach churned and her throat spasmed. "And the other arms?"

"Human trafficking . . . specifically children."

"I don't know anything about stolen art and definitely nothing about children." Issi put two shaking hands up in the air.

"I know." Thomas smiled reassuringly.

Issi didn't press him for a detailed description as a shadow passed across the man's face. There was a lot more ugly involved here than she needed to know about.

"Why me, and what is it you believe I can help you with? I'm still trying to figure out how Ma—Doyle found me." She shrugged then accepted the glass of juice from his wife.

"Well, I think I may have uncovered evidence that could explain how this man weaseled his way into your life. But first I need to know if you have ever dealt with any of these people?"

Thomas slid a manila envelope out from beneath his laptop. From it he pulled three photographs. Two were men of Middle-Eastern appearance, and the third was a woman with shocking red hair.

"Do you recognize any of them?" Thomas asked.

"I don't know the men, but her—I know her. I've met her . . . when I attended an exhibition at her gallery here in Noosa. Why? And what has it got to do with my art and . . ."

Issi considered Thomas then Tristan as her breakfast tumbled and lurched in her belly.

"These men are two Syrian nationals, brothers, and the head of their family business. I've been trying to get to the bottom of this for months now. The first man, Mohammed Eid, specializes in human trafficking. But this man, Farid Eid, is the one who Doyle would have had contact with. He runs the stolen antiquities side of the business." Thomas sat back and pointed to the photos. "They are the kingpins and their reach is global."

Issi gripped the edge of the table with her fingers. "And Desire is part of it?"

Thomas nodded. "Yes. Doyle and this woman, Desire Deveroux, have been using artists and her art galleries, which are spread out across Australia and Indonesia, to smuggle stolen art."

"Me?" Issi squeaked.

"Hey, Issi, breathe. It's okay." Tristan placed a hand on her back and drew her attention to him and away from her encroaching panic attack.

"Here, sniff this. It helps clear the mind." Rochelle passed Tristan a small dark brown glass bottle. "Open it and bring it to her nose." Rochelle demonstrated what she meant.

"What is it?" Tristan asked defensively.

"Plain old peppermint oil. It'll settle any nausea she might be feeling too."

Issi met Tristan's gaze as he passed the bottle under her nose. "Slowly now." He guided her as she inhaled through her nose.

The intense menthol aroma sprinted up her nostrils and drew a cool blanket of calm across her brain that spread into her stomach.

"Wow. That really works. Thanks." She smiled at Rochelle as she squeezed Tristan's hand.

Thomas shifted in his seat. "All good?"

Issi nodded. "How was I used? Or do you believe me to be involved?"

"No and yes. I am sorry. The beautiful tiger you created . . ." Thomas pulled a fourth photo from the envelope. ". . . was used as a cover for this." He presented another image.

Issi gasped. In the photo stood her tiger and beside it . . . "Is that a Dvarapala statue?" She pointed to the round-bellied gargoyle-like gatekeeper holding a *gada,* or mace, in its grasp.

"Yes. It's dated back to between the twelfth and fourteenth century and was lost at a dig a few months back ago near Prambaran."

"But how did my sculpture camouflage this?" Issi waved a shaky hand over the photographs.

"It has to do with the way they were packed in the crate."

The memory of the large crate the moving company had used when they'd collected the sculptures.

"The smaller statue was hidden beneath the tiger and between all the sawdust and other paraphernalia placed in the box to protect your sculpture. The customs official merely glanced inside."

"And x-raying?"

"Only done if suspicions are raised, which they usually are not thanks to lax officials and cash exchanging hands."

"And my tiger was 'bought' by one of these two men?" Issi's rising anger clawed its way up her throat.

"I am afraid so."

"Bastard!" She slapped the small table with her flat hand, causing everyone to jump. "Sorry." It was best she place both hands under her butt and take a deep breath. "How do you think I was involved?"

Thomas squared his shoulders, glanced at his wife, who nodded slowly, then turned his sharp gaze on her. "At first, we thought you were in on it with him. But when we discovered your true identity, and that essentially you had no memory beyond the bomb blast, we realized there was more to it. A fortnight ago, we finally got the CCTV footage salvaged from the day of the blast in Munich International." Thomas paused and considered her. "He's a master manipulator and according to our profiler, probably has sociopathic tendencies."

"What exactly is that?" Tristan spoke up as he shuffled his chair closer to Issi's.

"A person, as I've mentioned, who is a great manipulator, a charmer extraordinaire, lies like a trooper, and has no sense of guilt. They are capable of vile acts and wouldn't think twice about killing to get what they want," Rochelle explained.

Issi digested the explanation provided by Rochelle. Her stomach flipped and her mouth dried. Had she truly been that blind to Mark's charms?

"Don't blame yourself. You're one of half a dozen great artists being played by these decrepit criminals." Thomas's eyebrows drew together as he let go of a deep breath.

Tristan turned to face her. "He never hurt you, Issi, did he?"

"No, never."

Rochelle leaned across the table and placed her open hand on it, palm up. Issi straightened, took in another deep breath, then laid her hand in the doctor's.

"You cannot be angry at yourself. For goodness' sake, you were in the most vulnerable position any human could find themselves in and this man took full advantage of that." Rochelle squeezed her hand then sat back.

Issi delivered a look of determination to her husband, then folded her arms across her chest. "Tell me, how did he find me?"

12

————

Issi's head throbbed slightly as she made her way back to the table from the bathroom. While the peppermint oil had eased her stomach, a subtle nausea still slithered around inside her belly.

"The answer lies in the footage received from the Munich authorities," Thomas said as he tapped away on his laptop.

Issi sat and took another sip of juice.

Tristan leaned forward. "Footage of what?"

"Of the day the bomb went off and you lost your memory . . ." Thomas's voice trailed into the distance and Issi bit her bottom lip.

"Shall we take a moment?" Rochelle proffered.

"No. I'll be okay." Issi assured everyone and Rochelle gave her husband the all-clear.

"First of all, I need some background. Tristan, had Doyle ever met Issi before that day?" Thomas asked as he clicked and shuffled his laptop mouse.

Tristan inhaled deeply as he brushed a hand over his cropped hair. "Yeah. He'd been to our place once. I wasn't happy about having him there but we'd invited the whole brigade for a feed before our final deployment. He was part of our unit, whether we liked him or not. We weren't about singling any of our own out, no matter how weird they came across."

"And it was on this final deployment that he ambushed the brigade?" Thomas stopped tampering with his computer and looked directly at Tristan.

"Yeah, he and his band of terrorists."

Issi shivered as his fists clenched and his lips paled.

"It was at this Bbq, he was his usual withdrawn self, only interacting if spoken to. But then he changed when Issi showed her face. He couldn't stop looking at her, asking her if he could help in the kitchen, flattering her to the point where I wanted to confront him. He even promised to connect you with some important people in the art world when we returned. It also freaked you out, and you're the most tolerant person I know." Tristan turned his head and stroked a hand down her arm before leaving it to rest on her left knee. "On deployment, I walked in on him in my bunker one day. He said he'd found my wallet in the dirt, that I must have dropped it and he was returning it. I knew he was lying. When I searched my wallet, the photo I kept of Issi was missing. There was no way I could prove it was him without causing a ruckus. I needed mine and my men's heads strapped on straight for the mission."

"How long ago was this?" Thomas asked.

"A year before the . . . bomb." Tristan's shoulders dropped and curled around his chest.

"The Doyle you're describing doesn't match the Mark I know." Issi stood and walked to the open balcony doors of the room, wrapping her arms around herself. "Sorry." She turned to face the trio at the table.

"Don't be. He used the fact you lost your memory completely to his advantage." Rochelle spoke.

"He had photos of our engagement in Bali. How..."

Issi kept her gaze focused on Tristan. He was clenching and opening his fists as his left leg bounced up and down.

"Images are easily manipulated with the program these days." Thomas replied.

She walked back to where her husband sat. "I never understood why, but I couldn't love him. As much as I was grateful for him sticking around, for taking care of me, my art, the business . . . I never loved him. Every time he pushed for more, it felt wrong."

Tristan rose from his seat and pulled her into a strong warm embrace. He said nothing, only held her. In his arms, Issi felt that she was home, safe and loved, even if she couldn't remember their shared past.

"I'm sorry to end this moment. But shall we watch the footage?" Thomas interrupted.

Tristan let go and the pair sat.

"Let's get this over with." Issi positioned herself so that they could both see the screen as Thomas turned the laptop to face them.

"This is when we first see Doyle entering the airport. He was using the alias Mark Cornwall at this time," Thomas explained as they watched the grey grainy image of Doyle making his way past travelers and through check in.

"Who is the woman he sits beside?" Tristan pointed to the fuzzy figure of Doyle as he sat in a row of seats not far from where she and Tristan were.

Thomas shifted. "Isabella Irish. The woman whose identity he stole and used for you, Issi. We're not sure if she was directly involved or simply being used to create art as a front for the smuggling."

The woman shifted in her seat so that the camera caught her profile as she stroked Doyle's face intimately.

"She looks a hell of a lot..." Tristan pointed a shaking index finger at the computer.

"Like me!" Issi gasped.

"Yes, the resemblance to Isolde is uncanny." Thomas added.Issi kept her eyes glued to the screen, afraid she might dissolve into a puddle of hysteria if she moved. Tristan's body stiffened.

A few silent moments ensued before Thomas shifted in his seat again and clicked his mouse. Two rows away sat Tristan and Issi, none the wiser.

A flush of heat smacked her cheeks when the footage showed Tristan leaning in and kissing her. Her hair was longer then, halfway down her back. Though the footage wasn't clear, a blind person could have spotted their adoration for each other. She had truly loved this man, and he her.

She glanced at her husband's lips as he sat beside her, then turned back to the screen. A flutter of excitement spread across her body and a part of her longed for him to do it again.

On the footage, Tristan stood up and walked away

"That was when I left to pop into the bathroom." Tristan tapped his index finger on the screen.

Doyle turned around. The Issi in the footage looked to her left and the pair spotted one another.

"I recognized him." She sat forward and squinted at the screen.

"And he you." Tristan shook his head.

They watched as a smirk spread across Doyle's face. It appeared she spoke to him. He picked up his bag and walked off.

"I followed him?" Issi shifted forward on her seat.

"Yeah. And I assume you must have tried to SMS Tristan to let him know you'd seen Doyle. See here, this is where you pull your phone from your back pocket, and then ..."

A flash lit up the screen and the camera died.

Issi's world spun and blacked out.

"Just breathe." Rochelle laid a cool wet washer on the back of Issi's neck where she sat on the chair with her head between her legs.

"Feeling better?" Tristan whispered.

"Yes. No more black spots." Issi tried to smile as she slowly straightened.

"Maybe it's enough for one day?" Rochelle said rather insistently.

"No. I want to know it all. I've been living in a box without holes for two years." Issi waved as Tristan removed the wet washer.

"You've just experienced a huge breakthrough. I'm worried it might be too much." Rochelle stood, hands on her hips, looking down at Issi.

"How is it I can feel the heat, smell the smoke, but still not remember?" Issi reached for her glass of juice and finished what was left of it. Her head throbbed like a thousand horses' hooves trampling the earth. But she wouldn't tell any of them. No more waiting.

"Smell has a strong link to memories. You have an acquired brain injury—this is different to mere amnesia." Rochelle refilled everyone's glasses. "Okay, we can proceed slowly but if I think it's getting too much, I'm invoking my right to halt proceedings."

Issi nodded.

"Are Doyle and the bomb connected?" Tristan placed

the washer on the table before him as he retook his seat beside Issi.

"No. A terrorist organization claimed that right. It would seem Doyle was as stunned as anyone." Thomas clicked the mouse on a German paper headline and translated.

"As far as we can tell from information gathered, Doyle was travelling with Isabella so he had both their passports on his body. Isabella remained behind and was incinerated in the blast. Issi took a knock from flying debris and Doyle had just entered the nearby kiosk." Thomas flicked through images of the aftermath and the different locations. "Here is footage taken by a survivor on his phone." Thomas clicked the laptop again. The camera zoomed in on the chaos then paused as he froze it. On the screen, Doyle was sitting grasping an unconscious and bleeding Isolde in his arms, his face covered in soot.

"Doyle must have spotted Issi—"

"Where were you?" She cocked her head before glancing at Tristan.

"Trapped in the bathroom. The emergency service only got to us about thirty minutes after the blast." Tristan's shoulders dropped.

Thomas added. "Incidentally, the fact that you went to the restroom and Issi spotted Doyle ultimately saved both your lives."

13

THEY LEFT THOMAS CAMPBELL'S HOTEL IN A STATE OF SHOCK.

Issi sat in the front seat of the car. She pinched both hands between her knees and stared out the front window as parents and teenagers, toddlers and locals strolled by enjoying the summer sun and holiday spirit which Hastings Street epitomized.

Tristan didn't start the car immediately. Instead he leaned his head against the rest and wiped both hands over his face.

"By the way, does Doyle have remote access to the gates and your apartment?"

Issi shook her head. "Only Jeff and Sam."

"You never gave the man you were supposedly engaged to a key to your house?" Tristan turned in his car seat to face her. His eyes wild, his expression relieved.

"He asked. I always made the excuse that I'd be home to buzz him in. I told you, with him, it never felt . . . right."

From the corner of her eye, she caught Tristan's nod before the car engine purred to life.

"Do we need to be careful of him now?" she asked as she clicked her seat belt in.

"Yes. Best to carry on as though we have no idea where he is, but to keep in mind that he could be watching us," Tristan explained as he pulled onto the road from the parking lot.

"Oh." The memory of the man in a hoodie and cap sent a chill trickling down her spine.

"Just stay alert. Keep your doors locked. Tell me if you see something, anything out of place."

"Like flowers at my front door?" She teased.

"Touché." He shook his head as a large grin spread across his face. "You've not been home in a week. Do you need some groceries?"

"Yeah, that's a good idea."

Tristan pulled into the local IGA parking lot, and Issi's mind bolted at the thought of Sam or Jeff suffering because of her. Would this pretender try and harm her friends . . . would Mark be the sort of man to run or to stay hidden in the shadows?

———

Walking out of the store half an hour later with a loaded trolley, Tristan stopped. "Wait here. I need to pop into the bottle shop."

Issi smiled as he disappeared inside and she waited. It wasn't long before he returned with a box full of bottles.

"Not that I think we'll drink it all in one shot." He winked and smiled, offering up the single awesome dimple on the cleft of his chin.

"After all that we were shown today . . . I might just try," she replied. And they both burst out laughing.

The drive home was quiet. Sarah Caldwell played in the background and Issi contemplated the gravity of the information they'd received.

At the gate of her complex, she dug into her purse for the remote when Tristan gave her a sheepish glance and lifted a remote of his own.

"You've rented a unit here?" She wasn't sure how to feel about that, but it made sense when she thought about the flowers. And some part of her was slightly relieved at the thought that he wasn't far away.

"I owe you an explanation." He placed both hands on the wheel and drove to her apartment.

"Let's first get inside, settle, and pour some of that wine you bought." She tried for a smile.

Tristan turned off the engine and kept his eyes focused ahead of him.

"I keep thinking of that footage . . . If I'd stayed . . ."

"No ifs. We'd both be dead now. It's twisted, but what happened saved us both." She opened her door. "Come, let's get this stuff inside.

Tristan grabbed her bag and the box of wine as Issi gripped as many shopping bags as she could and the pair made their way up the stairs.

With all the groceries packed away, Issi excused herself. "I need to see a man about a dog after all those glasses of juice."

"Your mom says that all the time," Tristan replied.

Issi smiled nervously and closed the bedroom door behind her.

Tristan's words resonated deep inside of her as she washed then dried her hands on a small towel. *My mom . . .* her gaze fell on her drawer of lost yesterdays and she picked up the ring.

She wasn't ready to show him yet, but she was also tired of hiding it away. Issi lifted the lid of a small wooden jewellery box and took out a long silver chain. She threaded the ring onto it and placed it around her neck. The chain was long enough to tuck it inside her top and hide it from sight.

She wandered into the kitchen where she opened a cupboard from which she took out two glasses. Placing them on the bench, she then poured for each of them.

The pair sat out on her balcony as the sun set behind the apartment, draping the ocean in a dappled carpet of water sprites and magentas.

"Do you think now would be a good time to tell me how you found out I was still alive?" she asked, downed her glass of South Australian Semillon, then poured another.

Tristan leaned forward and placed his elbows on his knees, clasping his half-filled wine glass between his hands as he continued to gaze out over the view from heaven. "Okay, but I need to start from the day I—I lost you." His voice cracked.

"Okay." Issi placed a hand his arm. A zing of heat swirled in her center and pooled in places she'd thought numb and cold. Tristan shifted uncomfortably in his chair as his nostrils flared and his lips reddened.

Issi lifted her hand but he quickly caught it and held onto her.

"We—Miranda, Gus, her hubby, you, and me—we traveled to South Africa for your dad's funeral." Tristan leaned closer.

A painful stab caused her to clutch her chest. When she'd said goodbye as Isabella to parents she'd never known, she'd not felt a thing. But the thought of losing her dad, a man whose face she couldn't recall, sliced deep into her soul.

"Do you need a moment?" Tristan asked.

"No. But it hurts. I can't remember them and the thought I'll never see my father again . . ."

"You were close, the two of you, and you shared a special bond because of your art."

"The painting!" She jumped up from her chair.

Tristan gave her a strange look.

"This one." She pointed to the canvas in her living room.

No wonder she had felt such a strong attraction to it. Her world tumbled and dimmed as a pair of arms folded around her. For a moment, Issi rested her head on the hard, warm body behind her just as she had relaxed into his arms that day in the ocean. Her left hand instinctively stroked her chest where her ring nestled safely against her skin. The scent of his lavender and sandalwood cologne drifted into her nose and comforted her insides.

"Where did you find that?" Tristan's voice swept over her from behind.

"A few months back I was at a market with the guys. Sam happened on this stall run by a South African woman. Behind her, on an easel, stood this painting. I wasn't sure why, but I had to have it." Issi stepped out from his embrace and toward the painting.

Tristan followed. "This was one of his favorites. Except for the ones he gave you, I never expected any others would make it to Australia."

"I have more of his work?" Her heart ached and thrummed with excitement simultaneously.

"Yup. You have them hanging inside our house and your studio." Tristan stroked a hand over her cheek.

Issi turned from the painting to him, tears rolling down her cheeks.

Our house... My studio... a life lost.

His expression was a myriad of thoughts, feelings, and desires. Her heart lurched and her blood quickened.

"I never believed you died. Something inside of me felt you, saw you in my dreams. Everyone said it was part of the grieving process—denial, they called it." He kept his gaze fixed on the artwork hanging from her wall.

Issi cupped his face in her hands. Pushing on the tips of her toes, she brought his head to hers and pressed her lips against his. Tristan's arms wrapped around her as his hands travelled over her back, guiding her into his body.

His tongue gently parted her lips and began to stroke and taste the inside of her mouth. Issi reciprocated, finding her hunger for him increasing by the second. Her palms slid along his neck and came to rest on his chest. Her nipples puckered and protruded from her blouse. Tristan's hands moved and cupped her face, breaking their passionate embrace.

"God, I missed your taste, the feel of you." He stroked a thumb across her well-kissed lips.

"I need to know more, please?" She didn't want to end their kissing, but she wanted to recover as much as she could about them and that day, before she allowed herself to get any closer—although she already had an inkling that that ship had sailed.

Tristan took her hand in his and led them back to the patio. "The guys, my mates . . . our mates . . . were tired of me moping about. I'd changed—lost my love for life and almost farmed a harvest into failure. They got together and dragged my ass off to Melbourne for a lad's weekend and some footy. That was where I saw it . . ."

"Saw what?" Issi gripped his hand tighter.

"The billboard with your sculpture on it. It advertised an exhibition at a White Sails Gallery. But that sculpture, the one of the hand cupping a bunch of grapes, the charismatic angles and the flow—it was you. I knew it. I built you your own studio out at Blanchflower . . . our farm. Tourists would stop for a tour, some wine, lunch, and always . . . always they would end up buying those beautiful pieces you'd crafted with those beautiful hands of yours."

His gaze focused on her hands, now holding his. After lifting them to his face, he gently kissed first her left then her right palm.

"I thought either someone was imitating your style or . . . I went straight to the gallery and found out who the artist was. I stormed out thinking you had lied to me, run away—how could you?"

Issi pulled away and straightened.

"But when all the confusion settled, I knew there had to be an explanation. So, I returned and bought the piece. I had it sent to Blanchflower, then I flew to the Sunshine Coast."

Issi considered Tristan's confession. "I can't begin to imagine how you must have felt or feel."

Tristan sat as silently Issi gripped the wine bottle then poured them each another glass.

"Why'd you not come straight to my door? Why all the games?"

"I was planning to. But you strolled right past me one day on the boardwalk." A flash of pain crossed his face.

"I did?" Issi lifted her glass but didn't drink.

"Yup. The day before I saw you at the café."

almost choking on her mouthful of Semillon, she placed

her glass on the table and stared at him. "The scent of your cologne hit me so hard."

"Yeah I wasn't sure what happened there. I knew you didn't recognize me from a bar of soap. Damn near almost broke me in half." He took another sip.

Issi stretched across and took his free hand in hers. "I am so sorry."

"It's not your fault. When I realized you had no memory of me, I called a friend. Cynthia—a psychiatrist and a good mate of ours. She explained that if it was you, and you had suffered a cranial trauma due to the blast, it was possible you had memory issues. She suggested I should take my time. She told me the shock of approaching you all at once might be too much for you."

The flowers, the day at the café, and the poem?

Her mind had begged her to see what was right before her but her brain had simply refused. A thrum echoed across the inside of her skull and she instinctively rubbed the scar behind her left ear.

"It wasn't long after the day at the café that Thomas made contact and confirmed what I'd assumed. So, I reckoned I'd try to get you to remember, bit by bit." His shoulders slumped as he wiped both hands over his face then looked at her. "It's the hardest, scariest thing I've ever had to do in my life—besides burying you."

The air in her lungs froze as tears trickled down his face. Their stark beauty crystalized the golds and greens in his eyes, and a memory of long ago drifted to the surface. The smile, his gaze, his warm lips on her neck . . .

"Seeing you stand there, on the water's edge . . . You were alive and I couldn't run up to you and hold you, kiss you, smell you, tell you how much I missed you and longed for you. It was surreal. It was a dream." The grief on his face was too much for her to bear. Never had she seen love and loss shine as bright as it did on this man's face.

"But it was you." He wiped a hand across his eyes. Issi's heart broke as he continued.

"I had to let you go when everything in me screamed for me to run to you. To blurt it all out. To beg you to remember me."

Issi leaned back as she digested her husband's confession. Would she wake up in the morning and find that this was all a dream, one long surreal trick of her imagination?

She reached for her glass and sipped again. "Why'd you run away after you pulled me from the ocean?" Issi wrapped her arms around herself. The air was sticky, but she felt cold.

"I saw Doyle pull up behind the ambulance. I didn't want him to know I'd found you yet." He twirled his glass between his thumb and index finger, his gaze darting from it to her.

"And the pissing competition on the beach?" She wanted to, no, needed to understand why he had gone about things the way he had.

Tristan sighed, gripped his glass and downed it in one go, then wiped his mouth. "I'm no pro at this, Issi. All I knew was I was running out of time and had to get you to remember. On the one hand, I had a professional telling me to take it slowly and on the other, there was Interpol and Doyle. And until that day on the beach, I really had no idea how close the two of you were."

"What changed your mind?"

Tristan pushed back his chair, faced the ocean, hands on hips then turned back. A pale grey hugged both his cheeks and his eyes shone like twin bonfires, "The way you stared at him from the back of the ambulance—you hated him and I had left you alone with him."

An electric silence drifted into their conversation. It was Tristan who broke it.

"Look, I know my part in all of this has not been a hundred percent honest, but I did the best I could with what I had."

She should have been furious—kicked him out of her home. Who did he think he was, playing these games with her life? Issi glugged the last of her wine then aimed a heated look in his direction. Tristan was not a man who was out only to please himself. He was broken, a shell of his former self, searching for the better piece of the both of them. This man saw the part of her she no longer could. He knew her work simply from a picture on a billboard. Clearly, they were of one soul—ripped in half by an act of terror.

Issi clenched her eyes and willed her brain to remember, but it would not.

14

OVER THE DAYS THAT FOLLOWED, ISSI SPENT TIME WITH Tristan while they waited for an update from Thomas as to what their next step would be. They made an effort to breakfast at the café and spend some time with the guys in the mornings, then chatted and walked, or swam when they weren't at her place.

"Who's taking care of the vineyard while you're away?" she asked as they strolled along the sand of point Arkwright beach.

"We have a great property manager—an old army buddy who needed a hand after being honorably discharged. Plus, I have my laptop and can take care of the administrative side from anywhere." A soft smile spread across his face highlighting his features and sending a ripple of heat through her body.

"Are you in a hurry to get back?"

"We have all the time we need, Issi." Her husband assured her.

But something in his voice told her he was desperate to return home, and that he wanted her with him.

Was she willing to leave the life she'd forged for herself here? Would she manage to fit into the one she'd lost on Blanchflower? Her hand brushed over her shirt, touching the slight bump her ring made where it hung from its chain.

They made their way to her apartment. Tristan had brought a photo album along. The eerie feeling that had been haunting her the last few weeks returned—like she was being watched, and she often caught Tristan stopping to look around. But she put it down to the Interpol agent keeping tabs on them. She'd not seen or heard from Doyle since the day at the beach and assumed he'd bolted across the ocean to the safety of his crim friends in the Middle East.

"Juice?" Issi offered as Tristan closed and locked the front door.

"Sure," he replied and went to sit in the living room with the photo album on his lap. He was determined to share every detail of their past with her and though it overwhelmed her sometimes, she was relieved to finally be able to fill the void in her head.

"You'll like this one." Tristan held up the album covered in roses and honeysuckle. The first page had a photo of a younger, happier her and Tristan. Her hair was longer and he was dressed in his army uniform.

There were family photos of her as a little girl in South Africa and as a teenager on the back of his bike in South Australia. Both of them had broad smiles painted across their faces. Photos of her mom and dad, and her sister's wedding.

"You look a lot like your mom, but you have your father's demeanor." Tristan pointed to the photo of a man standing tall and proud beside Issi in her graduation gown. His hair was grey and thinning, but unlike other men of his age, he did not sport a belly.

"And how is my demeanor?" she asked inquisitively.

"Of course, he was an artist, though his talent lay more in farming the perfect grape. But you both have a habit of daydreaming. He's the one who wrote you that poem for your sixteenth birthday."

"The one about daydreaming?"

"One and the same." Tristan flipped the page.

Issi took a moment to let that settle in her mind. Her father had written her the poem.

"You okay?" He placed a warm hand on her shoulder and squeezed.

"Yes. I just wish I could remember more of him. He sounds so wonderful." She wiped a tear from her eye with the back of her hand.

"He loved you and your sister very much."

Tristan flipped to the last page. "I took this out of our album."

"May I?" Issi gripped the photobook and slid it onto her lap.

It was on the page with their wedding photo. Her gaze drank in the image of her, dressed in a halter-neck ivory gown with a pearl tiara holding a long gold lace-trimmed veil in place. Tristan was clean-shaven, in his formal army uniform, and as handsome as ever. The pair sat on the back of a horse-drawn cart, each wearing a besotted expression of joy and love. Layers of ivory fell like a waterfall around her, and she held a bouquet of forget-me-nots.

Something else caught her gaze.

"Was this my wedding ring?" She tugged at the chain around her neck.

Tristan's eyes widened as his arms and shoulders stiffened. "You still have it?"

She nodded. "Ma—Doyle said it was my old engagement ring from him. He was constantly on me to get rid of it, promising to buy me a newer, nicer one."

Tristan pinched the ring between his thumb and index finger. "You designed this. The sapphire was from my great grandmother's pendant."

Issi glanced once more at the photo. "We were so in love." She dropped the ring inside her top.

Tristan's eyes followed it as it fell out of view, his expression hard to read. Then with a sigh, he took the album before closing it and tucking it between him and the couch.

"I believe we still are."

"And where will I fit into all of this?" Would she be able to slip back into a life he remembered but she did not? Did she want to?

"Where you belong? Back home with me."

A cornucopia of knotted emotions exploded in her chest. "Where I belong?" What was that supposed to mean? She had a life here, friends . . . "I have no idea where I belong at this stage, Tristan."

"You had . . . have a life back in Mildura too." Tristan stood and began to pace.

"But that life is gone," she began as her phone rang. Issi grabbed it off the table, stood, before walking toward the kitchen .

"Hello. Yes, this is she. Oh, hi." She turned to face Tristan and pulled a face as she pointed to her phone.

"*Who is it?*" Tristan mouthed.

"Ah, hold on, Desire. I want to turn down my television." Issi lied then clasped her phone to her chest.

"I'll call Thomas. Keep her talking," Tristan whispered.

Issi nodded and swallowed hard. "Yes, okay. No, um . . . yes, this afternoon at three? Okay, yes, sure." Issi dropped onto the couch and groaned.

"You okay?" Concern creased his forehead as he held his phone away from his face.

"No." She huffed.

"What she say?" he asked.

"She wants to meet me at three this afternoon about the Pratta's auction and asked if I know where Mark is because she can't get hold of him."

Tristan repeated the information to Thomas. "Okay. Yes, I understand." He ended the call.

"What?" Issi didn't like the look which swept across his face.

"He believes you might make the perfect bait for Doyle," Tristan said with confidence, but his eyes spoke of exactly the opposite.

"Would he still bite now he knows you've found me?"

"Yeah, Thomas believes that Doyle has more than just a schoolboy crush on you and he might act irrationally due to his obsession over you. They're sure he's not left the country, or the state for that fact." Tristan slipped his phone into his back pocket.

Issi sucked in a deep breath and sat on her couch. "Obsession?"

Tristan nodded.

"But Desire doesn't know where he is?"

"I reckon it's part of a rouse." Tristan replied.

She bent her knees and wrapped her arms around them, hugging her legs to her chest.

"What can you tell me about Desire Deveroux?" Tristan sat beside her.

"I've never really dealt with her all that much before. Ma

—argh! Doyle took care of all of that. I'm not sure I know how."

"You never went along with him or handled any of the deals?" Tristan squinted and cocked his head.

"Yes, but they always discussed things in private."

Tristan's eyes bored into hers. Issi squirmed in her seat. What was he searching for, or rather, who was he hoping to find? The Issi before the bomb? The daughter, artist, and wife of two years ago?

"You've changed." His voice was barely a whisper, but the words cut in to her heart.

"What's that supposed to mean?" She straightened her back.

"Okay, no offense." He raised his hands. "It's just hard to understand how you allowed him free rein. Back home, you let me accompany you with all your dealings . . . but . . ." He shrugged. His eyes twinkled and he smiled.

"But?" She pushed. Issi's fingers gripped the leather cushion of the couch. Her anger was tempered only by that bloody dimple of his. It'd be the death of her. "Well, what?"

"You always took care of your own business. In fact, you were painfully adamant about it."

"I—" How did she explain she'd simply let Mark wheel and deal? That she'd had no clue how or *what* to say when it came to selling her art? Now she thought on it, Mark had pushed the idea that she was better at sculpting than business.

"What if I'm no longer the Issi you lost that day?"

What if they were no longer meant to be?

She didn't like that one bit, but it was a distinct possibility.

Tristan searched her face then seemed to find what he was looking for. He reached out and tucked a lock of hair behind her ear. "You have changed, but you're still the same," Tristan said as he leaned forward.

Issi found herself drawn to him like a magnet. Her eyes fluttered closed when his lips touched hers. His kiss was soft and warm as he teased her mouth and his hand ran along her back and into her hair. Her right hand reached around and stopped his from touching her scar.

"Let me love you—all of you," he whispered into her good ear. "Forgive me for not being there to protect you." He cupped her face in both of his hands.

Her insides trembled as, for the first time, she imagined a world without Tristan in it, and the thought rocked her.

"Better to have died with you than to have lost you as I did," he said.

"But I'm here. We're here. It's not perfect, but surely we can . . ." She shifted her body closer to his.

Two blazing orbs held her captive. Their green darkened with flecks of amber edging the border of his irises. The air around them quickened as he leaned into her once again. His lips stroked her cheek and jaw, trailing down her neck, igniting her very core.

Issi's heart bounced around her chest and her stomach churned and dipped as if on a roller-coaster ride. She closed her eyes and bathed her senses in the beauty that was this man. This gorgeous, stubborn, strong man who'd moved heaven and earth to find her.

Her skin tingled in excitement as his fingers ran the length of her spine.

His free hand gently gripped her chin between his thumb and index finger as he pulled her closer. His tongue pushed past her lips and invited hers to do the same as their kiss deepened. Issi tumbled from the jagged edge she'd been navigating onto the sweet, soft clouds of desire. She imagined that this was how the sands of a dry river bed must feel when the rains came crashing down and soaked the earth in a soothing bliss.

Her apprehension gave way to her hunger as she gripped his T-shirt and tugged him closer.

Carefully, she twisted and slipped onto his lap to sit astride the man who now captivated every one of her senses. She wanted to taste more, see more, and feel more. His hard shaft pressed into the soft, wet part of her. Issi began to grind and rub as her fingers found their way under his shirt. Her fingers devoured the ropes and mounds of his taught muscles.

A knock at the door caused them both to jump.

"It's us. We brought food." Jeff's voice called.

"Timing sucks," Issi whispered, pressing her forehead against Tristan's.

He reluctantly let go of her as she slipped off his lap. "You have no idea how much I want you right now." His voice was hoarse and his gaze hot as he rose from the couch. "I'd better sort myself out. Can't say hi to your friends like this." He motioned towards the bulge in his shorts.

Issi groaned. "I'll need to set some boundaries with those two." She smiled, stood, and fixed her clothing. "I'll get the door."

15

Issi stared at herself in in the full-length mirror bolted to the inside of her bedroom cupboard. She slipped on her long, deep blue cotton dress and black leather sandals. The blue reflected her irises, sharpening the soft velvet glow of her licorice locks as they gathered around her face. With care, she tucked her ring-laden chain beneath the fabric and, wiping her hands over her torso, she ignored the distant thrum of an oncoming headache. She needed water —her mouth was as dry as dehydrated fruit.

Though she always wore a dress when visiting a gallery, today it was also the best piece of clothing she could find that would work with the obscure listening device Thomas wanted to hide on her person before the meeting.

Tristan's eyes widened as she stepped out of her bedroom.

"What? Is it too much?" She turned this way and that, checking that she hadn't accidently tucked a hem into her undies or something.

"You're beautiful." His voice came out husky.

An electric bolt shot through her center. "Oh . . . thanks."

"Ready?" He held out his hand, not taking his eyes off of her.

"As I'll ever be."

———

"CAN I HAVE A MOMENT?" Issi asked as the walls of the hotel room closed in around her. She made her way to the bathroom and leaned over the basin, focusing on the silver push-plug as the world around her rocked and tumbled. Opening the tap she splashed some water on her face, then grabbed a clean hand towel and dabbed it dry. Straightening, she took in her reflection as she once more fingered the pretty sparrow broach pinned to her left lapel.

A soft knock on the door drew her attention. "Come in."

"It's only me," Rochelle said as she opened the door and slipped inside.

A sharp ache stabbed the inside of her head. No, not now. No more headaches. Issi reached inside her purse for some Panadol. She wouldn't risk the strong stuff, not with what was at stake today.

"Here, this should help with the nerves." Rochelle grabbed one of the clean glasses and ran some water from the tap before pulling another brown glass bottle from her pocket.

"What is that?" Issi pointed to the liquid the doctor was now dripping into the water.

"Rescue Remedy. It's a herbal relaxant."

"For a doctor, you sure use a lot of alternate medicines." Issi took the offered glass and turned it this way and that.

"Agh, don't get me wrong, I'm no hippie, but there's some good stuff out there that's not necessarily chemical-based." Rochelle smiled.

Issi sighed. "Well, bottoms up." She downed the concoction. "Boy, that tastes like really bad whiskey." She wiped the back of her hand across her mouth.

"Yeah, never said it tasted good. Okay. Thomas wants to test the listening device in your broach. You ready?" Rochelle said as she opened the bathroom door and stuck her head out. "We're good to go."

"I still don't see why I need it. Tristan will be with me." Issi touched the tail of the pretty broach.

"It's for evidence. If she mentions anything useful, we can use it." Rochelle reassured her.

"Well then, can you hear me?" she asked.

"Loud and clear," Thomas shouted back from the room.

Issi followed Rochelle into the room where Thomas and Tristan sat at the small table.

"Why the gallery? I mean, won't he try to make contact in another way?" Issi asked again as Thomas briefed her and Tristan one last time.

"I believe he may be assessing his opponent. Also, the gallery might be the one place he believes he still has control over." Thomas nodded toward Tristan. "I doubt Doyle is in a rational frame of mind at present. If he were, he'd have gotten out of the country as soon as Tristan made him. His obsession with you is the key, Issi."

Tristan stepped forward. "I don't like that you lot are using her as bait."

"I get it, believe me. Interpol is working with your state and federal police and we have plain-clothed officers watching you both around the clock. Doyle won't get near either of you unless we want him to."

———

"Ms. Irish!" Desire Deveroux exclaimed as she trotted over to Tristan and Issi.

She'd judged the woman in her late fifties, but the bright red bob and tight-fitting dresses she wore gave off a powerful sex appeal dipped in style.

Issi held out her hand to greet the gallery owner. "It's good to see you, Desire. This is Tristan Rivalen—my new manager."

"Oh." Desire gave Tristan a cold once-over. "Whatever happened to Mark? He was so suave. I haven't so much as received a text from him in days."

Issi caught the flash of assessment crossing Desire's face as she eyed Tristan. It sickened her that woman could lie so easily.

"Mark has uh . . . he's moved on." Ugh, lies tasted like crap. "To be honest, I was hoping you may have an idea of where he might have headed off to? It's never good for an artist when their manager simply dumps them." Issi plastered the best *I'm concerned* frown she could muster across her face.

"Ah, yes, I understand. But rest assured, Arts by the Ocean wants to continue working with you," Desire confirmed.

How does she know?

"Wonderful! So you can deal with Tristan from here on out." It was hard to hide her contempt for the woman. But she swallowed her anger and proffered her most innocent smile.

"Yes, of course." Desire's grin snaked across her face. "It's good to meet you, Mr. Rivalen."

"And you." He reciprocated.

"Shall we discuss tomorrow's auction?" Desire guided

them to the center of the floor where the Pratta stood beneath lighting set to emphasize the colors and angles.

Issi's pride nosedived. The sculpture which represented some of her best work also reminded her of the sordid trafficking ring she'd unknowingly been assisting. Her talent had been used to mask an evil most foul—something she would never forgive Doyle or Desire for.

"Don't let what they've done rob you of your success," Tristan whispered into her ear as he placed an arm on her shoulder and squeezed.

"Shall we?" Desire motioned toward her office.

"Yes." He nodded to her. "Coming?" He waited for Issi.

"Mark usually took care of business without the artist." Desire's tone edged on condescending.

"Not anymore." Tristan, not looking at the gallery manger, took Issi's hand in his.

Issi lifted her chin and squared her shoulders. "Let's do this."

———

Issi stepped out the gallery doors and inhaled deeply. The sights, sounds, and colors of the yuppie seaside town of Noosa and its famous Hastings Street, washed over her. Relief and a touch of excitement flooded her veins—the auction was geared for the following night. "Is it normal to feel excited and afraid at the same time? I know we're out to catch a crook, but I can't wait to see what people think of my sculpture—is that vain?" She turned to Tristan.

"No, you're not, and absolutely. That sculpture of yours, by the way, is spectacular. And the way you took control of the situation in that office . . . that is the Issi I know." Tristan placed a soft kiss on her forehead sending a zing whipping across her chest and coming to pool between her legs.

"You don't think I upset Thomas's plans? Desire was definitely not keen on me being in charge." Issi leaned back.

"No. Though she was very cautious about what she said. I'm sure Doyle found some way to listen in." Tristan placed his hands on her shoulders.

"If he's still here."

"Oh, he's still around. Thomas's assessment of him is spot on." Tristan frowned then pulled his phone out from his pant pocket. "It's Thomas." He tapped the screen as they walked to where the car was parked a little way down the road.

"No worries. We'll catch up tomorrow before the auction." He ended the call.

"So, what now?" Issi asked

"We wait. We remain vigilant, and we keep on pretending that we think Doyle has left the country and that you're super excited about tomorrow night." Tristan pressed on the small black remote as they approached the hatchback.

"Well the second part's easy." Issi smiled.

He walked to the passenger door and opened it but Issi didn't climb in. "When do I get to meet my family?"

"The moment all of this is over." He stepped toward her and out and ran his hands through her hair, pulling the curls away to see her scar. She tried to step back, but he slipped the hand from her ear to cup her neck and held her in place.

She blushed.

"You don't have to be afraid of me seeing your scars, Issi. My vows are my oath. I am here for you no matter what." He again lifted the hair covering her scar. "Don't be afraid. It's me . . ." His Adam's apple bobbed up and down in his throat as his eyes took in her damaged earlobe, scalp, and neck. "I wasn't there when you needed me the most. All our life together, even before the army, you were the one who carried me—picked me up, calmed my demons, listened, but when . . ." His voice broke and Issi found herself moving closer until his hard chest pushed into hers, causing her nipples to harden and her breath snagged in her throat.

She ran her hands along his arms and under the short sleeves of his shirt. His shoulders bulged beneath her touch and his warm skin reminded her heart, that yes, this was her man. "How could you have known? We live in a time where too many people think the only way to make their point is through violence." She focused on his gaze.

The world around them ground to a halt. Even the breeze off the ocean had the decency to still for a few sparse moments. Embers reignited in the depth of her soul. She wanted this man with every spark of life in her body. Her heart thumped, reminding her that while she might not remember him, her soul did.

A stranger standing across the road drew her attention. His body was angled away from them and his head was lowered, arms hugging his chest. A panama hat and a pair of shades hid his face—but something about him sent a chill down her spine.

"What is it?" Tristan spun on his heel and looked in the direction she was staring.

"That man over there." She nodded in the stranger's direction. "There's something . . . argh, my mind is playing tricks on me." She rubbed the scar behind her ear.

Tristan's body stiffened as he stepped toward the road, getting ready to cross it. The man took one more look, then turned his head toward a woman stepping out of a bathing suit boutique. He matched his pace to her and took off before vanishing between the holidaymakers. "Damn it."

"I doubt it was him. He was waiting for that woman." Issi pointed in the direction the pair had walked.

"Or he spotted an opportunity." Tristan stretched his neck as though trying to catch one last glimpse of them.

"Come, there's a celebratory chai waiting for us at the café." She squeezed his arm to reassure herself more than him. She prayed Thomas and Tristan's instincts were off and that Mark was gone—but a small wary part of her knew they were correct in their suspicions.

"That's new." Tristan clenched his fists as he turned back to her.

"New?"

"Your love for chai, but I'm not complaining." He winked as she sat on the front seat and closed her door.

———

ISSI SLIPPED OFF the broach and put it inside her handbag as Jeff set the two Christmas-themed mugs filled with the spicy, frothy drink in front of them. He didn't say a word, only smiled and winked before running off to serve the chaos that was holidaymakers.

Tristan took a sip. "Mmm. This is good. I love the spice."

Sam stood, chef's hat skewed on his head, spatula in hand, watching from the door of the kitchen. Only when Jeff whispered something as he passed did Sam nod and squint at Tristan.

"I thought they were okay with me . . . with us?" Tristan asked as he nodded and smiled back at Sam who then vanished into his kitchen.

"We need to tell them something, anything. They know

something's up and I hate lying to them." Issi cupped her mug in both hands.

"You're not lying to them. You're simply not telling them everything." Tristan leaned back and folded his arms across his chest.

"It's not like we'd put them in any more danger. Doyle already knows them. And tomorrow night is not only huge for my career . . ." Issi stopped and slowed her breathing. "It's full of unknowns and I'm bloody scared." Issi hissed the last part to make her point.

"You're right. I'm sorry. It's just hard protecting you, while trying to find this fucker, and maintaining a semblance of control without making you feel like a pawn." Tristan sighed. "Fine. Let's get them over for dinner tonight." He shook his head as he rubbed his chin.

"Thanks." Issi smiled.

She'd not spent as much time with her mates as she always had and, while she knew they were giving her space to sort out her life with Tristan, Issi hated keeping them out of the loop. They were more than friends; they were family.

"Everything okay?" Jeff asked as he passed their table with a tray full of drinks.

"Yup. You two coming for dinner tonight?" she called after him.

"Absolutely." Jeff smiled as he handed out the drinks then made his way back to the bar, patting her shoulder as he passed. "See ya at seven."

Issi inhaled the hot summer ocean-soaked air as she let go of some of the tension filling her belly with lead. She sat so that she could see past Tristan, watching people mooching around the esplanade.

"I don't expect you to come running back home," Tristan said out of the blue.

Issi's head shot to the left as she considered him. The lead in her belly doubled in weight and her mouth dried. "How long are you willing to wait?" She gave him a deadpan look.

"As long as it takes." He finished his chai.

A sliver of frustration snaked its way into her heart. "What if I never remember?" She couldn't look at her husband as she asked this. Instead she stared into her mug. The sprinkles of spice entranced her as they sank into the froth. She willed the leftover crumbs of cinnamon to form a shape and tell her what lay in store for her and Tristan. She was no fortune-teller, but a single thought struck true.

You knew me better than I knew myself, Tristan Rivalen, but do you know me now?

"We'll cross that bridge when we get to it." Tristan reached across the table and took both her hands in his.

The callouses on his palms rubbed against hers as his thumbs stroked her skin igniting sparks and quickening her blood. Issi swallowed the wave of emotion threatening to come crashing over her. The weight of the ring burned the skin on her chest as though begging her to recollect.

Her life was a veritable puzzle. Some pieces were missing, and others she'd put back in place without even realizing their importance. But one question remained. Would Tristan accept it if the Issi of old never returned?

16

It was dusk by the time the guys arrived for dinner. Sitting outside on the balcony, Tristan and Issi used this time to update them on all they'd learned from Thomas Campbell.

"Holy fuck!" Sam exclaimed.

"And now you're bait? Well, we will be there tomorrow night with bells and whistles on," Jeff added, then downed his glass of wine.

Tristan's tone was even and calm as he explained, "You can't show that you know anything about what we've shared with you. But an extra set of eyes would definitely help. We have no idea what Doyle's next move is except that we think it will be to approach Issi."

"I knew he was a piece of shit." Jeff slapped his hand on his knee.

"Well, villains and traffickers aside, how you two coping with all of this?" The skin between Sam's eyes creased as his voice grew deep and low.

Issi sighed at the same moment as Tristan rested his head in his hands.

"That bad, huh?" Jeff spoke before the silence grew awkward.

"It's not bad . . . It's just a lot to cope with all at once." Issi took it upon herself to try and provide some sort of explanation.

"Well, we're here for the both of you. I can't begin to imagine the emotional stress you're coping with, but remember, you're not alone." Jeff reached forward and squeezed Issi's hand.

"I know. Thanks." A tear trickled down her cheek.

Gosh, she loved the guys so much.

———

TRISTAN PACKED the last of the dishes into the washer as Issi closed the door behind her mates. It was good to be back in her own home. And with Tristan close by, Doyle wouldn't dare return—she hoped.

"It's really stuffy in here without the air conditioner on," he said, then turned to face her.

"Yup, that's Queensland for you. It's not like this back at your . . . home?" She fumbled for the right word.

"Nope." He shook his head. "Though I must say I'm getting used to it and the view."

Tristan wrapped a strong arm around her, pulling her into him. It felt so good to be held by this man. Her husband. Her protector.

The hunger in her center grew in intensity. He was the lost part of her soul, that warm, sweet filling in the hollowness of her heart. But sometimes knowing something one couldn't remember was frightening.

She raised a hand and placed it on his shoulder, not sure if she wanted to wrap her arms around him or push him away. Everything was so confusing. Her body longed to reveal itself to him, but her mind balked. It would be like her first time. She'd not slept with a man since she'd lost her memory. What would he expect from her if they did?

His nose touched her cheek, his lips, warm, smooth, just grazing the edge of hers. The heat from his body burned her skin and sent electric shocks up and down hers.

God, it felt so good. Of all the places in the world, this was where she belonged without a doubt—in his arms.

"I don't know where to go from here, Issi. I've missed you so much," he said as he stroked her cheek with fingers rough from years of work. "To sit beside you and hear you speak, to hear you laugh, to take in your scent . . ." Tristan drew her into him.

His kiss was desperate, hungry, and delicious. Issi let go and gave herself to him as she opened her mouth and allowed his tongue to explore every inch of her.

She took his hand in hers and led him to her bedroom. With care, she stood him so that the back of his legs touched the bed. Her hands shook, but she was determined to do this right.

Slowly, she unbuttoned his shirt then pushed it off his shoulders. It dropped off of his body as he sat and shifted back, pulling her onto him.

Her legs straddled him. God, he was glorious. Issi took a moment to trace the tips of her index fingers over the ropes of muscle on his arms, chest, and his abdomen.

Embers that had smoldered inside of her for days took flame as she cupped his face in her hands, leaned forward, and touched his lips with hers. His fingers danced across her bottom and tugged at her dress until they found their way and slipped beneath the soft cotton fabric and gripped the skin of her thighs.

Issi gasped as calloused palms rode up and stroked her back before making quick work of her bra and sending shockwaves through her system. Hungry lips devoured a path along her neck as one of his fingers traced its way from her spine to her breast and nipple.

Issi's need to feel more of him on her overrode all her senses. Tugging at her dress, she pulled it up and over her head.

Tristan's body froze as his hand rose and he fingered the ring, "I'll get this repaired."

She swallowed the lump forming in her throat, "I'd like that." Then leaned in and kissed him.

Tristan ran the tip of his tongue across her collarbone and down her breast before laving her peaked nipple.

"Tristan," she pleaded as he loved her breasts and shuddered when he let go and laid on the bed to study her. His eyes were on fire and his lips the color of rubies.

Issi greedily devoured the sight before her as his hands travelled the length of her midriff and landed on the curve between her thighs. His thumbs brushed lightly over the soft hairs covering her folds. Tristan raised his head, his eyes seeking her permission.

"Please," she whispered hoarsely.

He parted her folds and stroked their insides. Issi's world lit up as her hands gripped the covers. The tip of one thumb played with her. His head lowered, pushing her to the edge of insanity as his tongue flicked and loved her completely. His wet hungry mouth worked its' way up to hers. Her legs folded around his torso as she pushed her need against him.

He parted her folds and stroked their insides. Issi's world lit up as her hands gripped the covers. The tip of one thumb played with her. His head lowered, pushing her to the edge of insanity as his tongue flicked and loved her completely.

His wet hungry mouth worked its way up to hers. Her legs folded around his torso as she pushed her need against him.

"Your turn." Her voice hung heavy with need and hunger. Her fingers found their way to Tristan's zipper. They fumbled, but at last she managed to undo the damnable thing. It popped open to reveal the hard length of muscle that pushed against her inner thigh.

Her fingers stroked his wet tip poking out from the edge of his underwear, eliciting a guttural groan from him. A knowing of what they shared took hold of Issi, as she followed her instincts.

She couldn't resist. Planting her mouth in the crook of his neck, she began to trail a path of kisses from the pulsating vein beneath his ear and across his toned chest, tasting the firm skin of his abdomen only to stop just above his belly button.

Raising her head just enough for him to see her, she ran her tongue across her lips.

"Oh, dear God, Issi," Tristan moaned as both his hands combed through her hair.

Sliding back, she leaned in and removed his pants and undies before stroking the tip of her tongue from the base of his shaft to the very wet hard tip. She tasted him, licked him, and devoured him.

"Oh, fuck!" he exclaimed, and sucked in a breath through his teeth.

With care, he pulled her away and she shimmied up his body like a starved nymph. Their lips mashed together in a sweet, seductive mix of passion and one another. Hands rushed to explore, and teeth nipped and smoothed over sensitive flesh. Groans drifted off into the air as desire flared.

Tristan grabbed her and swung them around, placing Issi on the bed beneath him. He leaned back and stared.

"Is something the matter?" she asked nervously.

Tristan shook his head. "I don't know how to describe how often I've dreamed of this moment since I first saw you. I never believed I'd ever hold you again, let alone touch you." A single tear dropped from his face onto her left breast before he leaned in and continued his exploration of her.

His hands and mouth left a trail of burning flesh as they travelled along her neck and enjoyed each breast before moving onto her stomach, until he reached her panties.

His gaze didn't leave hers for a second as he slowly parted her legs.

"You are my goddess, my beating heart and my world."

Issi stared at the man who'd confessed his love for her time and time again. Who'd never forgotten her, even when she'd forgotten him. He was the most beautiful sight she'd ever seen. Strong, hard, and scarred like her.

He knelt, but instead of covering her with his body, he placed his hands on the bridge of her feet and slid them up, up, over her knee, shifting them to touch the inside of her thighs until one hand reached her center. His eyes held her gaze as his fingers parted her wet, hungry womanhood and stroked the sensitive flesh.

Issi's desire intensified, and she was certain it would turn her to ash as his fingers slipped inside and worked her lust into a frenzied need. Her back arched and her mouth fell open. "Tristan." His name fell from her lips as her passion peaked and pushed her to the edge of heaven. And then the warmth of his body disappeared.

"Don't go anywhere." His voice was hoarse and lined with urgency.

A packet ripped before Tristan fitted a condom. *Thank goodness one of them could still think straight.*

"You okay?" he wiped a stray lock from her face.

Not able to think straight she nodded and gripped his buttocks.

He slipped between her legs and pushed them farther apart with his. He positioned himself so his tip stroked her opening.

"Aaaah, please, Tristan."

His hungry grin exposed the dimples she'd grown so fond of.

He leaned forward and kissed her deeply. She liked to think that his hunger made sure she understood who her lips belonged to. Then he plunged his full length into her, pulled out slowly, and plunged in again. His movements grew in hunger and desperation. Issi pulled him into her. She wanted more. Deeper. "Harder!"

They were soaring above the earth, floating in space, picking stars off the Milky Way and flinging them across the galaxy. Tristan slowed as he rested his full weight on his elbows. "I don't want it to end just yet," he whispered, then placed his lips on hers and softly took what she had to offer as he rode her.

Digging her fingers into his flanks she begged, "More."

Tristan drove himself fully into her, drew back, and picked up the pace. Issi shifted her bottom and wrapped both legs around his torso.

In an explosion of pure ecstasy, they toppled over and fell back to earth, landing on a cloud of angel feathers. Issi clung to Tristan as his body shuddered from his climax. With her legs still wrapped around him, she turned her head and planted kisses in the crook of his neck.

This was everything she'd ever dreamed of and so much more. It was, she suspected, how every girl imagined her first time to be . . . *except this isn't my first time?*

Tristan pulled back, his gaze still hot and hungry. But

there was something else swimming in those golden-green orbs. They seemed to search hers, looking for the Issi who wasn't there.

The fact that such a soul-connecting experience was unable to elicit any memory, or at least hint at something they'd shared in the past, washed away the beauty of what they'd just shared and filled her heart with a cold fear.

17

Tristan leaned on an elbow and traced a finger around the bottom of her breast. He didn't say a word, but the smile and twinkle in his eyes spoke volumes.

"Thirsty?" Issi asked.

He leaned forward and planted one last kiss on her neck before grabbing his boxers and shorts. "Juice or water?"

"Water please . . . Was it . . ." She searched his face which was half hidden in shadow.

Tristan knelt on the bed beside her, stroking a thumb and forefinger across her forehead and the side of her face. "Perfect. Amazing. Spectacular." He sealed his promise with a kiss.

A breeze picked up off the ocean and pushed through the open window and curtain in her bedroom. Slivers of silver followed the breeze and caressed his face.

"And you?" The question sat bold and painful in his eyes.

Oh, God, what was she supposed to say? *Perfect. Amazing. Spectacular . . . but I still don't remember?*

Issi swallowed leaned against the headboard.

"Do you think you will ever remember us?" Tristan's Adam's apple bobbed up and down.

"Us?" She folded her arms around her chest. "You were hoping that making love would clear the last of the mist, magically repair my brain and hand me back my memory . . . Is that why—"

"No, yes . . . both. I know you felt our connection, our chemistry." Tristan sighed. "Perhaps if we found a good doctor?"

Issi stilled the prickling fingers of frustration Tristan's questions awoke. "I've seen the best of the best, Tristan. The ones in Europe before I left Munich. There's nothing that can be done."

"And what about the specialist Rochelle suggested?" His voice swam in hope, crushing her heart.

While she was excited by the offer, she knew better than him the hardship and letdown of maybes and broken possibilities the doctors always gave. "Yes, there is that. But there is no cure, Tristan. My brain is damaged, broken, and unlike a bone. It's not something that can grow back to the way it was before."

"But we have to try. Why won't you just try?" he pleaded.

Issi glared at him as she gripped the sheet around her and got off the bed. "It is what it is, Tristan. I was told I might remember some things, or I might remember nothing. As it stands, I'm only granted glimpses. Flashes. Broken bits and pieces, drips and drabs of what once was. Who I was . . . and no longer am."

Tristan placed both hands on her shoulders. "I'd hoped . . . when you saw me, and after we shared ourselves again, you might . . ." His grip intensified. "It would all come back . . ."

God, it was so frustrating to watch him search for a

woman who no longer existed. When would he accept that the Issi of his world truly was dead?

She pulled away. "A piece of metal pierced my skull and killed a part of my brain. Those memories are gone. I'm lucky to be alive. Do I need to draw you a picture?" She flinched as her words slapped this man who was her husband, lover, and the only person who knew her deepest self before the bomb—and who now felt out of place in her life. "I'm lucky I'm okay. Yes, I don't have any memory. Yes, I don't remember *your* home . . . *your* Isolde and *our* life before . . . all of this. But a part of me, a part more important than my stupid damaged brain, knows us! It knew us that first day you sat opposite me at the coffee shop. It knew us the day I painted your eyes onto that canvas! But . . ."

"But?" His voice trembled and the façade of the strong digger who held their world together slipped and allowed Issi a glimpse of the man inside. Alone, broken, and afraid, just as she was.

"But I wonder if that's enough?" She hated herself for saying it, but someone had to.

Tristan turned away from her, then bent and collected his clothes. He dressed and walked out of the room, leaving Issi alone with her anger.

Dropping the sheet, she walked over to her closet and pulled out a T-shirt and a pair of shorts, then stomped into her lounge.

Tristan stood on the balcony, hands in his pockets, and stared up at the sky which now boasted a pregnant moon. He banged the palm of his hand against the balustrade. "Dammit all!"

Issi stood frozen. Should she tell him it would all work out? They'd be okay? But how could she do that if she herself wasn't certain? There was a connection between them, that she could not deny, but was it enough to bring them back together? She gripped the ring beneath her shirt, then slipped the chain off her neck.

He was a decent man and she was damaged goods. Her heart screamed for her to grasp the straws of her past, but her mind, the one who saw a man who deserved a new chance with a whole love, told her to turn and walk away. Walk away from a past she no longer remembered. Walk away from a man who clearly loved her as much as she loved him . . . Yes, she loved him. But she wasn't convinced what she felt was enough to make up for who she no longer was.

Issi gripped her hands together. "I don't think this can work. Too much of the woman you loved has gone. I might look like her, but I no longer think that I am her." She slipped the chain over her head and removed the ring. She walked toward him, her legs feeling as though they were wading through quick-sand and placed the ring into the palm of his hand.

Tristan glanced at the ring, then at her. "Yes, you are. You are my everything, Issi. For two years, I have lived half a life. I cannot imagine a future without you."

"You deserve better. You've already buried me. I'll never be the girl you once loved. I'm broken, shards of the woman you once knew. I don't remember. I will never remember. This is my home now." She wiped the tears from her eyes with the back of her trembling hand and took a step back when he tried to reach for her.

"I don't care, Issi. You are my heart and my soul. Without you . . ."

"You are better off without me," was all she could muster. "Please leave."

Tristan shook his head. "No."

"Yes." And for the second time since she'd met him, Issi pointed toward the door for her husband to leave.

This time, though, it broke her heart to do it.

She turned her back as his footsteps echoed through the hollow space in her chest. The door opened, a deep sigh echoed across the room followed by a *click* as it shut.

It was time Tristan accepted the woman he'd once loved was buried in the cemetery on his farm. Her heart broke a little more. She was right to have ended it, to have given him the chance of a better future. All she'd be was a burden, a shell of a love he hoped to rekindle. And while she had a new life here and friends who were like family, Issi had to accept that without Tristan, it would be a very empty life from here on out.

18

THE SUN BARELY CRACKED ITS SHELL WHEN A KOOKABURRA sounded off the alarm. A new day had dawned. Hot, sticky . . . and sad.

Issi plodded to her studio, the hollow in her center growing with every step. She carried the painting of the eyes. She placed it facing the wall. It was time to buckle down and get to work. But her thoughts battled with her heart. Coffee and a walk would clear the fog suffocating her mind.

By the time Issi had sorted out her studio, showered, and had a second cuppa, it was time to call the GOMA. From now on, she would be her own manager. She was the queen of her own destiny, albeit a broken one. And when tonight was over she was going to fly down to Mildura and meet her family.

"Ah, Ms. Irish, yes, we weren't sure what was happening as my assistant has not heard back from your manager in over a week." The smooth tone of the GOMA director's voice echoed from her phone.

"I am sorry for the breakdown in communications, sir.

But I'll be handling all my own business from now on. Mark is no longer in the picture, and . . ." She sat on the high chair in her studio. The thought of Tristan not being by her side only fed the emptiness growing within her. "I'll be working under the new name of Isolde Rivalen."

"Oh. Well, that is a lot to deal with on your own, Mrs. Rivalen. Are you sure? I know of many agents who would be willing to take on an artist of your caliber."

Ugh, the man reminded her of Mark.

"I am sure. I'll be in touch. Your assistant has my email and mobile number. Good day, Mr. Forsythe."

Issi switched on an overhead lamp and stared at the blank sketch pad.

Every bone in her body ached for her to walk to Tristan's rental across the way from hers and beg for him to forgive her silly outburst—to plead with him for a second chance.

No, that was her heart speaking, egged on by her fear of ending up alone and unloved.

Issi picked up her piece of charcoal and began to work on her idea for the exhibition.

Anxiety gnawed at her insides. She would need to let the guys know what had happened and that she'd be going without Tristan to the auction tonight. Issi hadn't told him *not* to come, but she had sent him away—so why would he bother?

Oh shucks . . . She'd also need to let Thomas know. After picking up her phone, she texted the Interpol agent. She would see this through, get Ma- Doyle out of her life once and for all, then get on with it.

Issi dropped her head into her open hands, the charcoal pressing against her forehead. *Argh.* She wasn't one for complications and now that was all her life was about.

Squeezing the charcoal between her fingers until it

crumbled and broke, Issi tried to let go of her fear and pain. She wept for all she'd lost and had to sacrifice, and she wept because tonight was probably the night Doyle, the dipshit, would try to make his move. And now she needed to get through it without Tristan by her side.

She only had herself to blame for that.

19

LARGE YELLOW BANNERS HUNG ACROSS THE ENTRANCE AND above the sculpture advertising the charity and celebrating the evening. The organizers of the event had thanked her greatly for her time and donation.

"Isabella, I'd like for you to meet miss Yua Ito. She's a great fan of your work." Desire waved toward a beautifully dressed woman, with features of fine porcelain and smooth licorice tresses flowing down the length of her back.

"It's a pleasure to meet you Isabella." The woman held out a petite hand as she greeted her in perfect English.

"And I you."

"I've been following your work from the art galleries who have sold your pieces and decided I must fly to Australia to see them for myself." Yua explained.

Issi nodded as the Japanese woman tolerated interruptions from patrons and guests who wanted to meet the 'incredibly talented' Isabella Irish—she'd kept her name the same for this evening.

"I thought you said Tristan wasn't going to come?" Jeff whispered in her ear.

"Please excuse me." She smiled politely at the patrons surrounding her.

Issi touched the swallow broach on the lapel of her sapphire blue cocktail dress. It matched perfectly. She hoped it was working as well as it did the previous afternoon.

"What do you mean?" Issi frowned at Jeff who nodded in a direction over his shoulder. She spun around and came face-to-face with her husband who stood chatting to Desire Deveroux and another man she hadn't yet met.

Her breath froze in her throat and her thighs clenched together. Tristan could have passed for James Bond. He was clean-shaven and dressed to melt all the knickers in the gallery. Tuxedos suited him and so too did the debonair attitude he flung around like fairy dust.

Tristan cocked his head as his eyes found hers, and a smile like a thousand falling stars spread across his face. Her heart flipped and her mind screeched to a halt. How could she have driven him away in the manner she had? Nothing between them had changed. Her body knew him and reacted quite vigorously to his presence. Her heart ached for his lips to touch hers.

So her memory was stuffed. Her soul wasn't, and belatedly, she could never ignore what it was that bound them together—a love to withstand the ages. Love was everything, but in today's world and her with no memories of them, would it be enough?

"I didn't think he would after what I did last night," Issi replied quietly to her friend as she nodded a thank you to the waiter who'd brought a refilled champagne flute.

"Well, at least one of you has some sense." Sam strode over and joined Jeff and Issi. "I love you, girl, and you know it. But I hope after tonight, you sort your shit out. Surely there's a way forward for you both?"

She gave Sam an incredulous stare. "Not now please." And walked off to find out what Tristan and Desire were discussing so animatedly.

"Here's the artist of the hour." Desire's mouth pulled in a silly attempt at a smile which looked more like she'd smelled something nasty. Her eyes darted from Issi to Tristan and then around the gallery.

A thin sheen of sweat gathered on the woman's upper lip. A stormy ocean washed around Issi's insides. Desire was nervous, and that could mean that Doyle was nearby. Issi sipped her champagne hoping it'd take the edge off her nerves.

"You look beautiful as always." Tristan pulled her into him and gave her a warm hug.

"Thank you." Issi made sure to play along. She hugged him back.

"Okay, it's almost time," Desire said. "I've got a special spot for you to stand when the bidding begins. It's important our patrons see you while the auction takes place."

"Well, why don't you show us the ins and outs so we don't look like fledglings when everything happens." Tristan waved toward the Pratta.

"Oh, no. We can't have you standing with her. It's best you blend in with the crowd, get a feel for what's going on, perhaps urge the bid higher with one or two bluffs of your own." Desire gave Tristan the same crooked smile as she slipped her arms though Issi's. "Come, my dear."

Issi glanced back to where Tristan remained standing. Right now, she needed him by her side. But Tristan simply nodded in a way that told her he had this in hand.

Issis' gaze tripped nervously over the faces in the small crowd.

There was no sign of Doyle anywhere, but the iceberg that had formed in her center melted a little when the guys and Tristan stood close by. According to Thomas, there was a handful of plain-clothed policemen present at the auction too, but Issi wasn't able to pick them out.

"Ladies and gentlemen." Desire's voice boomed out across the gallery, drawing everyone's attention to them.

A tall man with a neat, silver fox look walked over to them.

"Isabella Irish, this is Janko Pretorius, our auctioneer." Desire said.

"Good evening, Miss Irish. What a lovely broach." His accent was clearly South African.

"Where is Mr. Clarke?" Desire whispered harshly.

"A bad case of the flu," Janko replied as he straightened his jacket.

"Well, he's one of the best." Desire's cheeks flushed, and Issi feared all may be lost.

"We are both well-known in the auctioneering circles, ma'am. But please, do embarrass both of us and call Mr. Clarke if you wish." The man's no-nonsense tone seemed to do the trick.

"Very well. Get on with it." Impatience rode Desire's voice and the auctioneer nodded politely.

———

"Sold!" A sharp crack echoed over the mumbling crowd as the auctioneer brought his gavel onto the sounding block. "For two hundred and five thousand Australian dollars."

Issi jumped then remembered to smile when the buyer

caught her eye and bowed respectfully. It was Yua Ito. Issi returned the gesture. Patrons' hands erupted in applause, accompanied by cheers and gasps.

This was the most any of her art had ever sold for. A thrill zinged through her body as her eyes searched for Tristan—she wanted to share this spectacular moment with him.

A cold hand gripped her arm.

"Come. There are papers to sign." Desire steered her away from the crowd before she could find Tristan or the guys.

"I—just . . . wait." She tried to pull out of the woman whose grip intensified.

"No time. This needs sorting out now." Desire led them to her office at the back.

"It'll take five minutes. I promise." This time Desire's red lips curled up in a more convincing smile.

Issi nodded and stepped inside when the gallery manageress opened the door and came face-to-face with Doyle. The once suave well-dressed man stood before her in a faded pair of boardshorts, a washed out T-shirt, and old trainers. He no longer smelled of expensive cologne, but instead desperation, and days' old sweat clung to him like a bad rash.

Issi's heart dropped to her toes at the same moment as her adrenaline spiked and her body readied to flee. But the world around her slowed as an arm gripped her waist and a cloth soaked in a sharp foul smell pressed against her mouth and nose. Issi tried to free herself from the molasses-like air which denied her a getaway. Smoke and fire, screams and shrills echoed across a void as her mind drew her back to a previous time she'd experienced danger.

Voices reverberated in the room around her . . .

"Did you get the car?"

"Yes. She's all yours. Now, just get her the fuck out of here before that stupid husband and his buddies find you!" Desire snapped, then shut the door.

Issi kicked back and managed to free herself momentarily. She lurched forward and grabbed at the handle but it'd been locked from the other side.

Before she could inhale and let out an almighty yelp for help, the arm snaked around her waist a second time. The vice grip forced her ribs inwards and a cloth pressed against her nose and mouth.

Using all her strength, Issi tried to fight free from her captor's grip but the effort caused her to suck in a breath. Her eyes burned and the sharp acrylic-like stench cut its way through her throat and into her lungs. Her vision blurred and her muscles began to lose their strength.

Issi turned her head this way and that in an attempt to rid herself of whatever it was that Mark had soaked the rag in.

"Shhh, babe. Don't fight it. It's for your own good. I've got you now. Shhh." His words twisted along her spine like a poisonous vine.

Issi closed her eyes and a memory, or a voice from one, surfaced as her body gave in to the drug.

"If you're ever attacked and can't fight free, just go limp—play dead. The moment you do that, the attacker relaxes, and in that split second you can break free." Tristan's voice from a day so very long ago echoed across time.

Issi didn't waste time thinking about it and relaxed completely. Something loud crashed somewhere nearby. Doyle let go and the last thing her spaced-out mind took in was a man shouting, breaking glass, and a hard thud to her head as she landed on the floor.

20

"ISSI, BREATHE, GIRL. PLEASE JUST BREATHE." A FAMILIAR voice echoed across the empty darkness.

A sharp slap stung her cheek and caused her to inhale deeply. Three loud cracks of thunder followed it.

"Is there a storm coming?" she asked groggily, trying to remember where she was and what she'd been doing and . . . "Why am I laying on the floor? Where am I?" She tried to push herself up as her eyelids peeled away from her eyes. "Whoa." She grabbed onto the body in front of her.

"Easy now. The ambo's on its way," the voice said.

"Ambo? Jeff, is that you?" She wiped a hand across her eyes and her vision began to settle. "Doyle!" The memory of his arm holding her against him as he pressed the rag to her face returned in a flash.

"The cops have gone after him. We found you just in time," Jeff explained as he sat on the carpet in front of her.

"Tristan?" She blinked.

"First, we need to get some oxygen into your lungs. I think he tried to put you out with ether," Jeff explained as the auctioneer ran into the office.

"Something's happened. You need to come quickly. Are you okay to stand?"

Sam stumbled into the office then knelt beside her and slipped an arm beneath hers before motioning to Jeff for help.

The world spun and for a second Issi thought the contents in her stomach might find their way back out of her mouth.

"Wh-what's happened?" She wiped a hand over her face as she found her balance and the room came to a standstill.

Sam gave her and Jeff a grave look. "It's Tristan ..."

―――――

Issi sat in the middle of the back seat so she could see through the front windscreen. She'd refused any help from the paramedics and made her mates drive her straight to the hospital.

Her knees shook as she wiped damp palms over them. The taste of the ether still swamped her mouth and dulled her senses.

Tristan had to be okay.

"Is this the fastest your car goes?" Issi shifted in her seat.

"If I go any faster, I'll either cause an accident or get a fine," Jeff exclaimed as he geared down, flicked on his indicator, and bypassed a large sedan.

Sam patted his partner on the leg. "Easy now, love." Then he turned to look at Issi. "Going slower and getting there in one piece won't change any sort of treatment the hospital will provide Tristan." His hand slipped from Jeff's leg to hers and squeezed.

"What happened?" Issi pinched her hands between her legs and closed her eyes. She deserved a chance to tell

Tristan what an immature idiot she'd been when she'd sent him packing.

"We saw that Desire vixen whisk you away the moment the hammer came crashing down. But by the time we'd made our way through the crowd, we spotted her halfway back to the auction area, alone. Tristan didn't give her a chance to lie to us. I must say, he's very persuasive when he's pissed." Sam shook his head and smiled. "Anyway, the door was locked and it took him and me to break it down. Doyle bolted through the window. Tristan ran to you first but Jeff told him to go after Doyle." Her best friend shook his head and wiped a hand across his face.

"It's not your fault." She reassured.

"I followed Tristan," Sam continued. "We ran after Doyle who'd made it down to the beach toward the nature reserve and into the bush. It was dark and we only had the moon to guide us. I tripped and twisted my ankle—Tristan caught up with Doyle. When I found them, they were struggling."

Issi clung to the front seat as Jeff took a sharp turn.

"I tried to help but copped a boot in the stomach. I think that's when Doyle grabbed whatever it was and stabbed Tristan." Sam grabbed the dashboard when Jeff swerved as a magpie swooped in front of the car.

"Fuck. I'm such an idiot," was all she could say when Sam's last words drove into her heart.

"It's all gonna be okay, lovely." Jeff assured her as he pulled up to the front of the hospital's entrance.

"We'll meet you inside," he called over his shoulder as she hopped out.

————

Issi slammed the car door shut and ran. Her ether-soaked limbs wouldn't listen and twice she stumbled. Her world dimmed and flickered, and she had to stop, breathe deeply, and force herself to walk as straight as she possibly could. The large glass doors to the emergency department of the new coastal hospital slid open. She skidded to a halt at the main reception desk. A girl she judged to be straight out of school looked up and smiled from behind the screen.

"Where is he?"

"Calm down, ma'am. How can I help you?"

Issi straightened and took a deep breath as Jeff and Sam came running behind her.

"My husband, Tristan Rivalen. They brought him here. He was attacked . . ." Her mouth battled to keep up with her words and some came out all twisted and upside down. The girl frowned and grabbed the phone beside her.

Jeff, obviously realizing what the receptionist must be thinking, stepped forward.

"She's in shock, not on drugs. Her husband is Tristan Rivalen. He was brought in only moments ago. A stab wound?"

The young woman replaced the receiver and turned her eyes to the computer screen, her fingers skipping across the keyboard.

"They're stabilizing him for surgery. You can wait here or upstairs in the theatre lounge."

———

The elevator opened. Two large white doors with a black engraved banner over the top reading *Theater Four* greeted Issi and the guys from across the passage.

"What now?" She shivered as she stepped out.

"We wait." Sam took her hand and led them to the lounge. They weren't alone. Hovering in the quiet space decorated with plastic chairs, a small television screen, and a table stacked with used magazines, stood two uniformed policemen.

Issi walked past them to the lady sitting behind a desk at the theater's entrance. "My husband, Tristan Rivalen—have they brought him up?" Issi clasped her shaking hands beneath her arms.

The woman smiled at the trio, then tapped her keyboard. "Yes. Only just. It'll be a while. Feel free to take a seat. There's a vending machine around the corner if you're hungry or thirsty."

"Mrs. Rivalen?" a young man dressed in Queensland police blues asked.

Issi nodded to the lady then turned her attention to the man. "Yes."

"I'm Constable Norton. I know this may be hard for you at present, but do you think you may be able to answer a few questions?"

"Sure." She shrugged as she walked over to the chairs, the guys taking a seat on either side of her.

"I need you to think. Where would the suspect go? Is there a special place he mentioned, or person?" The young constable asked.

As hard as Issi tried, she battled to focus on the information requested.

Issi shook her head. A distant throbbing made itself known. She'd soon be in the grips of a paralyzing migraine.

"You knew this man for two years and you barely know his habits? How is that possible?" The policeman pressed.

Issi's mind was lost in a waterfall of panic, guilt, and fear

—and didn't register the hint of suspicion in the young man's tone.

What if Tristan died? What if she never got to see him again and tell him what a fool she'd been? So what if her memories didn't repair. They could make new ones . . .

"Mrs. Rivalen."

"Can't you see she's in shock?" Jeff curled a protective arm around her.

"Sir, it's vital that we gather as much information as soon as possible," the young constable explained.

"Mrs. Riv—"

"Constable Norton," a short plump man ordered as he came to stand beside his young constable, Thomas and Rochelle beside him.

"This is Detective Inspector Campbell. Interpol will be leading this investigation from here on out."

"Come. You need to breathe. You didn't allow the para-medics to treat you and you still have that drug in your system." Rochelle waved Jeff out of the way then wrapped an arm around Issi's shoulders.

"I'll see if I can find us some decent coffee," Sam said. "Hands up for milk, sugar . . ."

He diligently took the orders then waltzed off along the corridor.

The doors to theatre slid open and a woman dressed in green scrubs walked out.

"Rivalen family?" she called out. Issi jumped, swayed, then sat back down as the woman walked over to her.

"Wife," was all Issi managed to say.

"We've stopped the internal bleeding and managed to clean out all the debris left behind from the branch. He's been taken to the intensive care unit. You can see him for a short bit and then he needs to rest. If he survives the night, then he should make a full recovery."

Relief washed over Issi. "*Thank eeew . . .*" her brain-to-mouth synapsis disintegrated and the world began to spin at light speed. The familiar stud of horses galloped through her skull, pounding her grey matter to dust. Her sight began to blink in and out. Voices dimmed, and her world blanked.

21

WITH EFFORT, SHE FORCED HER EYES OPEN. WHERE WAS SHE? A strange beeping sound echoed like a hundred chiming bells inside her skull. She winced. There was a cannula running from her hand to a bag hanging from a metal pole.

Memories flooded back.

"Where is . . ." Her voice cracked, and her tongue scrapped like sand paper in her mouth.

"Easy now." Jeff and Sam appeared out of nowhere and stood beside her.

"What happened to me? Where's Tristan?"

Sam grabbed the remote and pressed it, making the bed's head rise and move her into a sitting position. "He's in ICU."

A rush of relief washed over her. But, Sam's tone hadn't sounded too chipper. "What? What is it?"

Jeff sat as Sam remained standing.

"It doesn't look good," he said.

"B-but the woman—sh-she-said he would make a full recovery . . ." Issi struggled to comprehend what could have changed.

"They're not sure what happened but his . . . argh, what did they call it?" Jeff looked to Sam.

"His vitals." Sam filled in the gap.

"Yeah, his vitals began to weaken. They're not sure if there's an infection or more internal bleeding. For now, he is critical. Oh, and they found this in his hand." Jeff handed her a ring - *her wedding ring.*

The dam wall broke and emotions she'd kept locked away since waking up cold and alone in the hospital room in Munich collided everything Tristan had stirred. They slammed into the brick and mortar of her heart like a tsunami.

"Come now, come now." Jeff wrapped his arms around her, while Sam reached for the tissue box.

Issi plucked a few and wiped her eyes and blew her nose.

"I'm—such—an—idiot." She managed between sobs.

"No, lovely. You're a woman who has defied medicine and remembered the love of your life, not with your mind, but with your heart!" her mate assured her.

Issi embraced her two closest friends. "I love you both so much." She sobbed a little more.

"And we love you," they replied in unison.

"Where are the Campbells?" she asked.

"We told them we'd keep them updated. They've gone back to their hotel. Thomas needs to coordinate a search for Doyle." Sam shifted where he stood.

Issi nodded then straightened herself, slipped the ring back on her finger, and said, "Take me to Tristan! I have to see him now. Where are my shoes?" She searched the area as her bare feet hit the floor.

"You kicked them off in the car on the way over. Did you only realize that now?"

"Shit." She shook her head at herself as she brushed her hands over her creased dress. Her legs wobbled. "How long before this crap works out of my system?" she said to no one in particular.

"Soon, according to the nurse." Jeff answered. He grabbed a wheelchair after explaining the situation to the nurse on the emergency unit. The pair pushed Issi to the ICU.

At the door, the trio sanitized and signed in before the guys took her to Tristan's bed.

Jeff whispered into her ear, "We're just outside. We're going nowhere, okay?"

Issi nodded then turned her attention to the doctor who stood on the opposite side of the bed. His eyes were a dull green, rimmed by red. He'd clearly had a long day. Her gaze fell on his name tag: Dr Blacksail. A chill settled in her veins. He looked at her with compassion as he sighed and said, "We stopped the bleeding. Got to him in time, but . . ."

"What?" she asked, confused.

If they'd fixed him up, why was he fading?

She glanced at the beautiful man who had loved her so completely the night before. The same one she'd chased away. Two small pipes poked into his nostrils, while bags of fluid hung from a pole, dripping their contents into the clear tube sticking out of the crook of his arm. On his finger sat a square grey device with a grey cord snaking its way up to a machine which showed signs and symbols she did not understand. On his chest were more cords held down by electrodes.

"I've only ever seen this once before in my life. But that was a mother who'd lost her baby at birth. She'd simply given up."

Issi cocked her head. "Are you telling me he has lost his will to live?"

The doctor nodded. "He called for you when they wheeled him in. I've never heard a man so heartbroken, so worried, and devastated."

Oh, if only the doctor knew. It was because of her Tristan no longer wanted to live. She was too much of a coward to face the truth of her feelings. Instead she'd acted like a fool and shown him the door.

"Where was he . . ."

The doctor pointed to the back of his own torso as he explained, "Above his right kidney. Just missed the renal artery."

Anger welled inside of her. Doyle had obviously attacked Tristan from behind -- coward.

The doctor sighed then walked around to where Issi sat. "We've done all we can. The rest is up to him. My advice? Stay with him, talk to him, hold his hand. The subconscious is a strong thing. Perhaps if some part of him realizes you weren't harmed . . . well, who knows?" He shrugged and patted her on her shoulder before leaving.

There were three other beds with patients in them, but they were on the far side of the unit. Carefully, she got out the chair and lifted the sheet covering a very naked Tristan, then slipped in beside her husband. She made sure her presence did not interfere with the myriad of pipes, lines, and other tubes connected to him.

His body was cool, nothing like the heated one that had radiated in her bed. She laid her head on the pillow beside his and lifted his hand to her chest where she curled her fingers around his.

"But it's against policy." A female voice whispered behind her.

"Yes, but this is a special case, Nurse Oslo. Just leave them be; draw the curtain if you must. It's my direct order," the doctor instructed.

"Husband," Issi whispered.

She didn't know why she'd called him that, but some part of her brain had flicked a switch. This man who'd fought heaven and earth in denying her death had found her and brought her back to him. Now it was her turn to do the same.

"I'm here. Forgive me, please," she pleaded in a soft whisper as tears blurred her vision. "I was afraid. Stupid. Arrogant. I shouldn't have told you to go. Please don't leave me. I need you. I love you." She squeezed his hand tighter as she shifted her head and kissed his bare shoulder. "My brain doesn't remember, but my heart does. We can have so much fun making new memories. Without you in this world, there is nothing left for me."

Issi buried her head in the pillow and let go. She let go of her fear, her anger, and her utter frustration and help-lessness.

The nurse drew the curtain. She said nothing to Issi who lay curled around his sleeping body.

Tristan's head shifted slightly. Issi snuggled into him closely and drifted in and out of sleep as the residual ether began to tug her back into a black oblivion. Too tired to fight it, she allowed her mind to rest. But before sleep stole her away, her lips uttered her favorite quote. *"I don't know if life is greater than death. But love is more than either."*

————

A WARM HAND cupped the back of Issi's neck. "Hey, wife."

Her head snapped up, almost connecting her forehead with Tristan's teeth.

"Slowly now . . . argh," he groaned, lifting his arm.

Issi wiped the back of her hand across her blurry eyes. She was lying beside her husband. Careful not to cause him any more discomfort, she slid across and swung her legs off the bed. Making sure not to pull the sheet with her and minding his catheter pipe, she came to sit on the bed beside him.

"Well, it seems kangaroo nursing is as good for the big ones as it is for the wee bubs, eh?" A nurse with a soft brogue accent and a grey bob stood at the foot of the bed with Tristan's file in her hands. A girlish grin swept across her face as she said, "Probably best if yew sit back in the chair noo." The friendly nurse pointed to where the wheelchair still stood beside Tristan's bed. "His vitals improved not too long after you snuck into bed with him. Your two friends returned at sparrow's fart this morning. Haven't left the waiting area since." The nurse motioned with her chin toward the door of the unit.

Issi slid off the bed. Her legs felt sturdier this morning. "I clean forgot." She ran her fingers through her hair, forgetting about her scars. She yawned and stretched. "They were so worried about you," she said to her husband.

"Jeff and Sam?" Tristan asked, his throat sounding as dry as hers felt.

Issi nodded.

"You'd better go out and see them. I'll be fine," he added, clearly spotting her hesitation. "I'm not going anywhere."

"Why don't you go get a coffee in the downstairs café? And I was reminded to tell you to visit the ED for a checkup this morning. We must look at his wound and clean him up before doctor comes around. With any luck, it's straight to the medical ward for you today." She smiled at Tristan. "He's in good hands, my dear." The nurse's voice was as warm as her smile.

"I'll be right back. I just want . . ." Tears tumbled down her cheeks. "Oh, God, Tristan," she wrapped her arms around his neck, pulling loose his heart monitor cords and ripping the canula from her hand. The machine began to squeal and announce there was no beating heart. Issi didn't care.

"I'll never leave you again," she sobbed into his neck as the nurse righted the machine and placed a sticky dot plaster on her hand where the IV had been inserted.

"Nor I you." He gripped her free hand.

22

"I've let management know you'll be moving in with me but that we'll rent the apartment for the rest of the holiday," Issi said as she dropped Tristan's bag on the floor beside the kitchen counter.

"How are your folks handling not jumping on a plane and flying up?" Issi asked. Tristan had called them all after he'd been moved to the ward.

"I can be really persuasive. That, and I totally downplayed my injury." He winked. "Though my mom will rub it in until the end of days."

"Cool. Are they angry with me? I mean, you asked them to wait until you were discharged . . ."

"It wasn't easy, but they're happy to give us our space until you've reconnected with your family. Now, I suppose it's time we made that call?" He sat on the couch.

Issi swallowed and didn't look at him as she walked past and opened the doors leading to the balcony. A soft, cool breeze trickled inside and the fresh scent of rain drove away all her apprehension.

It'd started to drizzle early that morning when she'd

gone to collect Tristan from hospital. Everything was washed clean-the air fresh, and her life . . .

"FaceTime?" She sat beside him.

"Yeah." He tapped his phone screen.

Her mom and sister looked like younger and older versions of the same person. Issi's brain throbbed and her heart bulged.

"Lolo!" her mother exclaimed, using what Issi assumed was a pet name for her. "Oh, we are so blessed. When Tristan called us from the hospital . . . It's . . . it's been so hard not to jump on a plane and head straight up!" Her mom wept. The subtle South African accent stirred a long-forgotten something inside of Issi.

"Well, at first she didn't believe him. Issi. Passed on a few choice Afrikaans words too."

Miranda giggled when her mother clicked her tongue and said, "Haai is *nie!*"

"You sure did, Ma. No use in denying it."

Issi burst out laughing at her mother's denial in Afrikaans. It was as though there'd not been a moment's separation between them.

She chatted to her mother and sister until Tristan's phone battery flashed red. Her heart bulged with love and exuberance as she plugged the device in to charge and returned to her husband in the lounge.

"Thank you," she whispered into his neck, then planted a kiss on his cheek and then his lips.

"For what?"

"For finding me."

———

"BREATH, ISOLDE." Tristan used her full name as they stood at the arrivals gate of Brisbane Domestic terminal. "I don't need you passing out."

Issi focused on inhaling and exhaling as they waited for the arrival of her sister and mother.

His parents and Miranda's husband, Gus, and their daughter were due to fly up the following day.

The white-tinted glass doors opened, and Issi's heart jumped into her throat as people off the flight from Victoria filed through. Issi's eyes skipped over many faces but none belonged to her sister or mother.

She faced Tristan as a huge smile opened his face. Slowly, she turned back.

Standing just inside the doors were two women. One with a funky short style colored in an array of coppery-blond hues. Issi recognized the face as her own, only wiser. Beside her, Miranda—younger, taller, and built like she worked out, with long dark chocolate hair and soft grey eyes —even more so the spitting image of their mother.

"Isolde?" her mother whispered as she brought her hands to her mouth, blinking tears from her eyes.

Issi nodded as her own tears broke free from their restraints and tumbled down her face.

The women stood dead still as the doors opened and closed, hiding them then revealing them.

At last, they grabbed the handles of their suitcases and began to walk toward Issi and Tristan. Then, without warning, her mother dropped her case and ran. She collided with Issi, flinging her arms around her neck and sobbed. Issi's arms enfolded her mom and tightened like a vice grip. She smelled of honey and cinnamon and everything a mother should.

"I didn't believe it. I tried to, but I couldn't. Even when

we spoke yesterday— I told myself it must've been a dream!" Her mother spoke into her neck.

A second pair of arms joined the hug as Miranda held both her mother and her in a grip of steel. "Don't you ever leave us like that again," her sister's soft voice commanded.

"Never," Issi promised, even though she understood now more than ever that life was not hers to control.

———

Issi's apartment bulged with laughter and voices. She was sure it'd pop like an overripe grape with all the people who now moved, sat, and stood around in it. The guys had offered their café for the reunion celebration, but Tristan's mother had declined and said it would feel 'homelier here.'

Issi had simply smiled inwardly, rolling her eyes.

She looked on quietly from a corner of her home as the two moms fussed over the food. "We should probably warm up more pies, Suzanne." Harriette, Tristan's mom, pointed a finger at the frozen pastries on the counter.

Her mom sighed, then grabbed the box and dramatically tipped the pies onto an oven tray.

"Yes. They've always been this way—just in case you were wondering," Tristan whispered in her ear when Issi leaned back against a wall and considered the pair of matriarchs order, control, and organize their worlds.

"Some part of me knows that I missed it. This is what family's all about, isn't it?" She turned her head and basked in her husband's loving gaze.

"Sure is." He smiled, then kissed her gently.

Outside on the balcony, Rochelle and Miranda sat chatting, while Luka, Issi's niece, rolled around on the rug Issi had thrown down for her to play on.

Life. Was. Good.

Tristan's father, James, her brother-in-law, Gus, and the guys, including Thomas, sat in the lounge and swapped jokes.

"Hear about the guy who invented Lifesavers?" James asked before sipping his beer.

Jeff replied, "Yeah, they say he made a mint!"

Everyone broke out in full-bellied laughter.

"Your father sure loves him his dad jokes." Issi chuckled at the silly quip.

A warm silence fell over the apartment and everyone's attention turned toward Tristan and Isolde as though they still could not believe she was alive.

James stood, raising his tin of beer. "To the angel who was returned."

"Hear, hear!" Everyone chimed in and the last lost piece of Issi's heart found its way home.

23

IT HAD BEEN A BUSY FEW DAYS IN HER SMALL APARTMENT AT Point Arkwright. Gus, Miranda, and Luka were situated in her guest bedroom, while the old folks lived it up in the unit Tristan had originally rented across the way.

"Enjoy the beach." Issi waved her guests off as they made their way down the path toward the gate leading to the road and the boardwalk.

"Oh, and stop by the guys' café for lunch. You'll love the food," she added.

Once inside, she joined Tristan, Thomas, and Rochelle on the balcony.

"Thank you for the specialist's referral." Issi hugged Rochelle, then sat.

"It's no problem at all."

"You all packed and ready for your flight home tomorrow?" Tristan asked.

"Yeah. Just in time for Christmas. Goodness knows, Pa would never forgive us if we missed it." Rochelle laughed.

"What's it like, going back to a place that's so dangerous?" After everything they'd been through with Doyle, she wasn't sure how South Africans coped with the constant violence in their lives every day.

"Agh, I'm not sure how to explain it." Thomas leaned back in his chair. "We're used to it. To us, it's bad, but not as bad as it is to you. I sometimes think we're like lobsters in a pot. The water's gradually heating and once we realize it's boiling, it might be too late. But it's home and we love it."

"Well, if I've gotten anything out of all of this . . ." Issi waved her hand through the air. ". . . it's that if it's your time . . . it's your time. And it doesn't matter who or where you are. If your name is next on the Grim Reaper's list, you're a goner." She sighed deeply.

"So you're here to say goodbye and tell us what happened with Doyle?" Tristan broke the somber mood.

"My people, with the help of the federal police, who are fantastic by the way, caught up with Doyle in Kununurra early this morning," Thomas said.

"What happens to him now?" Issi asked.

"My 2IC will fly him to the Hague in the Netherlands for prosecution as soon as all the paperwork is completed and confirmed. He's been accused of art crimes, but they might show him leniency if he helps bring down the two heads of the trafficking circles," Thomas explained.

"Wow. I wonder if he will?" Issi mused out loud.

"Doyle Morhold's the sort who shows no loyalty and only thinks of his own ass. Trust me when I say he'll sing like a sugarbird being fed honey." Tristan smirked.

———

TRISTAN SHUT the front door as the Campbells left. With the apartment empty but for herself and Tristan, Issi wound her arms around his lean torso and inside his shirt.

"You're all healed?" She winked.

"Aww, this tiny scratch is nothing." Tristan patted the side of his body.

"It was more than a scratch." Issi peered around his back at the smaller bandage now covering the site.

"We'll need to take it easy, but there are only internal stitches left." He finished his sentence with a kiss on her lips, then leaned back and grinned.

The dimples on his face still affected her in a legs-turn-to-jelly kind of way, and she wondered if she'd ever tire of them.

She suspected not.

He kissed her forehead as his hands started to roam over her body.

Issi smiled. "I have two new commissions. One for White Sails in Melbourne and one for the lady who bought the Pratta."

"The one from Japan?" His hands stopped their exploring.

"Yup. Fancy a short holiday? I thought you and I could fly the piece to her when it's done."

"Every day's a holiday with you, wife." He pulled his phone from his pocket and tapped on the screen. "But we will need to stop off at the farm first. I need to make sure all is well there before I follow you around the globe."

"Do you mind if we make both the vineyard and the sunshine coast our home?" Issi searched his face as she asked a question which might be difficult to answer.

"As long as I am with you, I am home."

A familiar voice echoed from the speakers as Sarah Calder sang.

"Care for a dance?" He twirled her around.

"Always," she smiled.

Tristan stopped then cupped her face in his hands and brought her lips to his.

The urgency of his kisses had not lessened over the weeks. If anything, Issi suspected their bond had grown tenfold.

As they kissed, the verse of a poem by Lady Jane Wilde echoed in her mind.

> *'So loved Tristan and Isolde,*
> *In youth's sunny, golden time,*
> *In the brightness of their prime;*
> *Little dreaming hours would come,*
> *Like pale shadows from the tomb,*
> *When an open death of doom*
> *Had been still less hard to bear,*
> *Than the ghastly, cold despair*
> *Of those hidden vows, whose smart*
> *Pale the cheek, and break the heart.'*

"Death missed his mark this time around," she gently pulled away.

"What's that?"

Issi smiled and stroked his lips with the edge of her thumb. "Only that we must be the luckiest lovers on this earth."

The End

AFTERWORD

I've always been a sucker for a soppy romance. At a very young and impressionable age, my Nan read the woeful tale of Tristan and Isolde to me. The love of two souls separated by lust, lies, greed, and envy broke my heart, and I vowed that one day I would make it right by them. While *Forget Me Not* does not follow the plot of this ancient tale of star-crossed lovers, it is my dedication to them—my way of reuniting them and proving that death is not always victorious.

PS. I would like to extend my thanks to the awesome people, and the seaside town, of Coolum Beach, Mildura. Noosa and Constantia. I used some artistic license when describing scenes, and while some are similar there are times when a handful are not. This same license was once again applied when I described the jurisdiction and proto-cols of Interpol and the local police and ADF – who by the way I have a huge amount of love, time and respect for. Thank you for your dedication and sacrifice.

Also, a huge thank you to an amazing artist I met earlier

in 2019 at QPAC when I experienced the amazing magic of Celtic song and dance, Sarah Calderwood. Thank you for allowing me to mention you as Issi's favorite musician.

ABOUT THE AUTHOR

G'day, howzit, sanibonani, goeie dag.
My readers know me as Michelle Dalton and my friends, as the
call-a-spade-a-spade-South-African.
Originally from Pretoria, South Africa, Michelle Dalton and
her family fled the rising violence taking over her beloved
country and now lives near Brisbane, Australia with her
husband and triplet sons.
While juggling a nursing career and teenage sons, she loves
to escape into her fictional world. Michelle has a deep love
of horses and enjoys weaving them into dramatic stories
with honourable men and strong women.
Her other hobbies are gardening (usually trying to save her
precious herbs and bulbs from an overactive miniature Jack
Russell),
painting, and reading. She's also a huge Star Trek and
Marvel Comics fan, and as of recently a wee fan of DC too.

CONNECT WITH MICHELLE

http://michelledaltonauthor.com
michelle@michelledaltonauthor.com

SIMPLE TRUTHS

BOOK 1 IN THE LOST & FOUND SERIES

Can broken hearts ever love again?

https://amzn.to/3oGm7km

A stolen kiss beneath the stars followed by gut wrenching heartbreak, rips apart Rochelle Le Roux and Thomas Campbell's young lives.

But when their paths cross over a decade later, Rochelle fights the simple truth that maybe fate has brought them back together for a reason.

In a country fraught with danger, adversity, and cultural differences, can the long lost lovers grasp their destiny for a chance at re-claiming their happy ever after? Or will the pain of their past succeed in keeping them apart?

This thrilling, second chance love and romantic suspense, a 2019 ARRA nominated first book in the Lost and Found series, is a must read by bestselling author Michelle Dalton.

"Michelle weaves the universal experience of "love" with some indigenous-to-South Africa harsh realities, as she tells this very poignant love-story."

EPONA

BOOK 1 IN THE HIGHLANDS SERIES

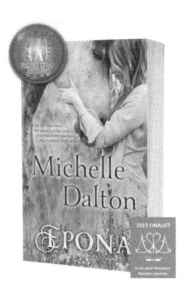

Can love heal all ?

https://amzn.to/3hlIwca

A farm attack robs Sadie Munro of her loved ones leaving her scarred and broken. Now her only hope is to escape the country of her birth for a foreign land, far away.

But Sadie's life may still be in danger.

Blane Buchan is an Englishmen seeking a life away from the emptiness of London society and a past he'd rather forget. His heart yearns for a woman who'll love him and not his status or bank account.

Sadie and Blanes paths cross unexpectedly when a mysterious mare appears out of nowhere.

Can Sadie overcome the trauma of her past and find redemption and love in the wild Scottish Highlands?

From the mountains of South Africa to the magical Highland Moors of Scotland, this is a story of redemption, love and the powerful connection between humans and horses.

VALA

BOOK 2 IN THE HIGHLANDS SERIES

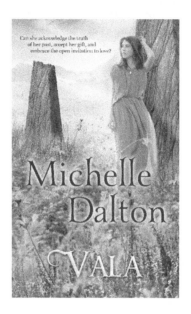

Is Love Enough, Or Will The Darkness Takeover?

https://amzn.to/3h53lKb

Can Calla acknowledge the truth of her past, accept her gift, and embrace an open invitation to love?

On the anniversary of her father's untimely death, forensic anthropologist, Doctor Calla Conroy, is thrown in the deep end of a murder investigation.

To complicate the situation, the voice in her head has returned.

With everything to lose and no time for a psychotic break, Calla ends up in the small highland's village of Lairg. Here she meets the handsome Detective Hamish Bell, who elicits powerful emotions that frighten her.

Can Calla make peace with her traumatic past and the reality of her gift? Or is she simply losing her mind, her heart, and possibly her career?

From the award winning author of Epona, comes the second in a thrilling women's fiction romance you won't be able to put down.